OTHELLO

William Shakespeare

Scene I

Venice. a Street

[*Enter RODERIGO and IAGO*]

RODERIGO

> Tush! never tell me; I take it much unkindly
> That thou, Iago, who hast had my purse
> As if the strings were thine, shouldst know of this.

IAGO

> 'Sblood, but you will not hear me:
> If ever I did dream of such a matter, Abhor me.

RODERIGO

> Thou told'st me thou didst hold him in thy hate.

IAGO

> Despise me, if I do not. Three great ones of the city, In personal
> suit to make me his lieutenant, Off–capp'd to him: and, by the
> faith of man,
> I know my price, I am worth no worse a place: But he; as
> loving his own pride and purposes, Evades them, with a
> bombast circumstance Horribly stuff'd with epithets of war;
> And, in conclusion,
> Nonsuits my mediators; for, 'Certes,' says he,
>
> 'I have already chose my officer.' And what
> was he?

Forsooth, a great arithmetician, One Michael
Cassio, a Florentine,
A fellow almost damn'd in a fair wife; That never set
a squadron in the field, Nor the division of a battle
knows
More than a spinster; unless the bookish theoric, Wherein the
toged consuls can propose
As masterly as he: mere prattle, without practise, Is all his
soldiership. But he, sir, had the election: And I, of whom his
eyes had seen the proof
At Rhodes, at Cyprus and on other grounds Christian and
heathen, must be be–lee'd and calm'd By debitor and creditor:
this counter–caster,
He, in good time, must his lieutenant be,
And I—God bless the mark!—his Moorship's ancient.

RODERIGO

By heaven, I rather would have been his hangman.

IAGO

Why, there's no remedy; 'tis the curse of service, Preferment
goes by letter and affection,
And not by old gradation, where each second Stood heir to the
first. Now, sir, be judge yourself, Whether I in any just term am
affined
To love the Moor.

RODERIGO

I would not follow him then.

IAGO

O, sir, content you; I follow him to serve my turn upon him: We cannot all be
masters, nor all masters Cannot be truly follow'd. You shall mark Many a
duteous and knee–crooking knave,

That, doting on his own obsequious bondage, Wears out his time, much like his master's ass, For nought but provender, and when he's old, cashier'd: Whip me such honest knaves. Others there are Who, trimm'd in forms and visages of duty, Keep yet their hearts attending on themselves, And, throwing but shows of service on their lords, Do well thrive by them and when they have lined their coats Do themselves homage: these fellows have some soul; And such a one do I profess myself. For, sir, It is as sure as you are Roderigo, Were I the Moor, I would not be Iago: In following him, I follow but myself; Heaven is my judge, not I for love and duty, But seeming so, for my peculiar end: For when my outward action doth demonstrate The native act and figure of my heart In compliment extern, 'tis not long after But I will wear my heart upon my sleeve For daws to peck at: I am not what I am.

RODERIGO

What a full fortune does the thicklips owe
If he can carry't thus!

IAGO

Call up her father,
Rouse him: make after him, poison his delight, Proclaim him
in the streets; incense her kinsmen, And, though he in a fertile
climate dwell,
Plague him with flies: though that his joy be joy, Yet throw
such changes of vexation on't,
As it may lose some colour.

RODERIGO

Here is her father's house; I'll call aloud.

IAGO

Do, with like timorous accent and dire yell
As when, by night and negligence, the fire

Is spied in populous cities.

RODERIGO

What, ho, Brabantio! Signior Brabantio, ho!

IAGO

Awake! what, ho, Brabantio! thieves! thieves! thieves! Look to your house, your daughter and your bags! Thieves! thieves!

BRABANTIO appears above, at a window

BRABANTIO

What is the reason of this terrible summons? What is the matter there?

RODERIGO

Signior, is all your family within?

IAGO

Are your doors lock'd?

BRABANTIO

Why, wherefore ask you this?

IAGO

'Zounds, sir, you're robb'd; for shame, put on your gown; Your heart is burst, you have lost half your soul; Even now, now, very now, an old black ram Is topping your white ewe. Arise, arise; Awake the snorting citizens with the bell, Or else the devil will make a grandsire of you: Arise, I say.

BRABANTIO

What, have you lost your wits?

RODERIGO

Most reverend signior, do you know my voice?

BRABANTIO

Not I what are you?

RODERIGO

My name is Roderigo.

BRABANTIO

The worser welcome:
I have charged thee not to haunt about my doors: In honest
plainness thou hast heard me say
My daughter is not for thee; and now, in madness, Being full of
supper and distempering draughts, Upon malicious bravery,
dost thou come
To start my quiet.

RODERIGO

Sir, sir, sir,—

BRABANTIO

But thou must needs be sure
My spirit and my place have in them power
To make this bitter to thee.

RODERIGO

Patience, good sir.

BRABANTIO

What tell'st thou me of robbing? this is Venice; My house is
not a grange.

RODERIGO

Most grave Brabantio,
In simple and pure soul I come to you.

IAGO

'Zounds, sir, you are one of those that will not serve God, if the devil bid
you. Because we come to do you service and you think we are ruffians,
you'll have your daughter covered with a Barbary horse; you'll have your
nephews neigh to you; you'll have coursers for cousins and gennets for
germans.

BRABANTIO

What profane wretch art thou?

IAGO

I am one, sir, that comes to tell you your daughter and the Moor are now
making the beast with two backs.

BRABANTIO

Thou art a villain.

IAGO

You are—a senator.

BRABANTIO

This thou shalt answer; I know thee, Roderigo.

RODERIGO

Sir, I will answer any thing. But, I beseech you,

If't be your pleasure and most wise consent, As partly I
find it is, that your fair daughter, At this odd–even and
dull watch o' the night, Transported, with no worse nor
better guard
But with a knave of common hire, a gondolier, To the gross
clasps of a lascivious Moor—
If this be known to you and your allowance,
We then have done you bold and saucy wrongs; But if you
know not this, my manners tell me We have your wrong
rebuke. Do not believe That, from the sense of all civility,
I thus would play and trifle with your reverence: Your
daughter, if you have not given her leave,
I say again, hath made a gross revolt; Tying her duty,
beauty, wit and fortunes In an extravagant and
wheeling stranger
Of here and every where. Straight satisfy yourself: If she be in
her chamber or your house,
Let loose on me the justice of the state
For thus deluding you.

BRABANTIO

Strike on the tinder, ho!
Give me a taper! call up all my people! This accident
is not unlike my dream: Belief of it oppresses me
already.
Light, I say! light! [*Exit above*]

IAGO

Farewell; for I must leave you:
It seems not meet, nor wholesome to my place, To be
produced—as, if I stay, I shall—
Against the Moor: for, I do know, the state,

However this may gall him with some cheque, Cannot with
safety cast him, for he's embark'd With such loud reason to
the Cyprus wars,
Which even now stand in act, that, for their souls, Another of
his fathom they have none,
To lead their business: in which regard, Though I do
hate him as I do hell–pains. Yet, for necessity of
present life,
I must show out a flag and sign of love,
Which is indeed but sign. That you shall surely find him, Lead to the
Sagittary the raised search;
And there will I be with him. So, farewell. [*Exit*]

[*Enter, below, BRABANTIO, and Servants with torches*]

BRABANTIO

It is too true an evil: gone she is;
And what's to come of my despised time Is nought but
bitterness. Now, Roderigo, Where didst thou see her? O
unhappy girl!
With the Moor, say'st thou? Who would be a father! How didst
thou know 'twas she? O she deceives me Past thought! What said
she to you? Get more tapers: Raise all my kindred. Are they
married, think you?

RODERIGO

Truly, I think they are.

BRABANTIO

O heaven! How got she out? O treason of the blood! Fathers, from
hence trust not your daughters' minds By what you see them act.
Is there not charms

By which the property of youth and maidhood May be abused? Have you not read, Roderigo, Of some such thing?

RODERIGO

Yes, sir, I have indeed.

BRABANTIO

Call up my brother. O, would you had had her! Some one way, some another. Do you know Where we may apprehend her and the Moor?

RODERIGO

I think I can discover him, if you please, To get good guard and go along with me.

BRABANTIO

Pray you, lead on. At every house I'll call;
I may command at most. Get weapons, ho! And raise some special officers of night. On, good Roderigo: I'll deserve your pains.

[*Exeunt*]

SCENE II

Another Street

[*Enter OTHELLO, IAGO, and Attendants with torches*]

IAGO

> Though in the trade of war I have slain men, Yet do I hold
> it very stuff o' the conscience To do no contrived murder:
> I lack iniquity
> Sometimes to do me service: nine or ten times
> I had thought to have yerk'd him here under the ribs.

OTHELLO

> 'Tis better as it is.

IAGO

> Nay, but he prated,
> And spoke such scurvy and provoking terms
> Against your honour
> That, with the little godliness I have,
> I did full hard forbear him. But, I pray you, sir, Are you fast
> married? Be assured of this,
> That the magnifico is much beloved, And hath in his
> effect a voice potential
> As double as the duke's: he will divorce you; Or put upon
> you what restraint and grievance The law, with all his
> might to enforce it on, Will give him cable.

OTHELLO

Let him do his spite:
My services which I have done the signiory
Shall out–tongue his complaints. 'Tis yet to know,— Which, when
I know that boasting is an honour,
I shall promulgate—I fetch my life and being From men of
royal siege, and my demerits May speak unbonneted to as
proud a fortune As this that I have reach'd: for know, Iago,
But that I love the gentle Desdemona,
I would not my unhoused free condition
Put into circumscription and confine
For the sea's worth. But, look! what lights come yond?

IAGO

Those are the raised father and his friends: You were
best go in.

OTHELLO

Not I I must be found:
My parts, my title and my perfect soul
Shall manifest me rightly. Is it they?

IAGO

By Janus, I think no.

[*Enter CASSIO, and certain Officers with torches*]

OTHELLO

The servants of the duke, and my lieutenant. The goodness
of the night upon you, friends! What is the news?

CASSIO

The duke does greet you, general,
And he requires your haste–post–haste appearance, Even on the
instant.

OTHELLO

What is the matter, think you?

CASSIO

Something from Cyprus as I may divine: It is a business of some heat: the
galleys Have sent a dozen sequent messengers This very night at one
another's heels, And many of the consuls, raised and met, Are at the duke's
already: you have been hotly call'd for; When, being not at your lodging to be
found, The senate hath sent about three several guests To search you out.

OTHELLO

'Tis well I am found by you.
I will but spend a word here in the house, And go with
you.

[*Exit*]

CASSIO

Ancient, what makes he here?

IAGO

'Faith, he to–night hath boarded a land carack: If it prove
lawful prize, he's made for ever.

CASSIO

I do not understand.

IAGO

He's married.

CASSIO

To who?

Re–enter OTHELLO

IAGO

Marry, to—Come, captain, will you go?

OTHELLO

Have with you.

CASSIO

Here comes another troop to seek for you.

IAGO

It is Brabantio. General, be advised; He comes to
bad intent.

[*Enter BRABANTIO, RODERIGO, and Officers with torches and weapons*]

OTHELLO

Holla! stand there!

RODERIGO

Signior, it is the Moor.

BRABANTIO

Down with him, thief!

They draw on both sides

IAGO

You, Roderigo! come, sir, I am for you.

OTHELLO

Keep up your bright swords, for the dew will rust them. Good
signior, you shall more command with years
Than with your weapons.

BRABANTIO

O thou foul thief, where hast thou stow'd my daughter? Damn'd as
thou art, thou hast enchanted her;
For I'll refer me to all things of sense,
If she in chains of magic were not bound, Whether a
maid so tender, fair and happy, So opposite to marriage
that she shunned The wealthy curled darlings of our
nation, Would ever have, to incur a general mock, Run
from her guardage to the sooty bosom
Of such a thing as thou, to fear, not to delight. Judge me the
world, if 'tis not gross in sense
That thou hast practised on her with foul charms, Abused her
delicate youth with drugs or minerals That weaken motion: I'll
have't disputed on;
'Tis probable and palpable to thinking.
I therefore apprehend and do attach thee
For an abuser of the world, a practiser Of arts
inhibited and out of warrant. Lay hold upon him: if
he do resist,

Subdue him at his peril.

OTHELLO

Hold your hands,

Both you of my inclining, and the rest:
Were it my cue to fight, I should have known it Without a
prompter. Where will you that I go To answer this your
charge?

BRABANTIO

To prison, till fit time
Of law and course of direct session
Call thee to answer.

OTHELLO

What if I do obey?
How may the duke be therewith satisfied, Whose
messengers are here about my side, Upon some present
business of the state
To bring me to him?

First Officer

'Tis true, most worthy signior;
The duke's in council and your noble self, I am sure, is
sent for.

BRABANTIO

How! the duke in council!
In this time of the night! Bring him away: Mine's not an
idle cause: the duke himself, Or any of my brothers of
the state,
Cannot but feel this wrong as 'twere their own; For if such
actions may have passage free, Bond–slaves and pagans shall
our statesmen be.

[*Exeunt*]

SCENE III

A Council-chamber

The DUKE and Senators sitting at a table; Officers attending

DUKE OF VENICE

There is no composition in these news
That gives them credit.

First Senator

Indeed, they are disproportion'd;
My letters say a hundred and seven galleys.

DUKE OF VENICE

And mine, a hundred and forty.

Second Senator

And mine, two hundred:
But though they jump not on a just account,— As in these
cases, where the aim reports,
'Tis oft with difference—yet do they all confirm
A Turkish fleet, and bearing up to Cyprus.

DUKE OF VENICE

Nay, it is possible enough to judgment: I do not so
secure me in the error,
But the main article I do approve
In fearful sense.

Sailor

[Within] What, ho! what, ho! what, ho!

First Officer

A messenger from the galleys. [*Enter a*

Sailor]

DUKE OF VENICE

Now, what's the business?

Sailor

The Turkish preparation makes for Rhodes; So was I bid
report here to the state
By Signior Angelo.

DUKE OF VENICE

How say you by this change?

First Senator

This cannot be,
By no assay of reason: 'tis a pageant,
To keep us in false gaze. When we consider
The importancy of Cyprus to the Turk, And let
ourselves again but understand,
That as it more concerns the Turk than Rhodes, So may he
with more facile question bear it,
For that it stands not in such warlike brace, But
altogether lacks the abilities
That Rhodes is dress'd in: if we make thought of this, We must not
think the Turk is so unskilful
To leave that latest which concerns him first, Neglecting
an attempt of ease and gain,

To wake and wage a danger profitless.

DUKE OF VENICE

Nay, in all confidence, he's not for Rhodes.

First Officer

Here is more news. [*Enter a*

Messenger] **Messenger**

The Ottomites, reverend and gracious,
Steering with due course towards the isle of Rhodes, Have there
injointed them with an after fleet.

First Senator

Ay, so I thought. How many, as you guess?

Messenger

Of thirty sail: and now they do restem
Their backward course, bearing with frank appearance
Their purposes toward Cyprus. Signior Montano, Your trusty
and most valiant servitor,
With his free duty recommends you thus, And prays
you to believe him.

DUKE OF VENICE

'Tis certain, then, for Cyprus. Marcus Luccicos, is
not he in town?

First Senator

He's now in Florence.

DUKE OF VENICE

Write from us to him; post–post–haste dispatch.

First Senator

Here comes Brabantio and the valiant Moor.

[*Enter BRABANTIO, OTHELLO, IAGO, RODERIGO, and Officers*]

DUKE OF VENICE

Valiant Othello, we must straight employ you
Against the general enemy Ottoman.

To BRABANTIO

I did not see you; welcome, gentle signior;
We lack'd your counsel and your help tonight.

BRABANTIO

So did I yours. Good your grace, pardon me; Neither my
place nor aught I heard of business
Hath raised me from my bed, nor doth the general care
Take hold on me, for my particular grief Is of so flood–
gate and o'erbearing nature That it engluts and swallows
other sorrows And it is still itself.

DUKE OF VENICE

Why, what's the matter?

BRABANTIO

My daughter! O, my daughter!

DUKE OF VENICE

Senator

Dead?

BRABANTIO

Ay, to me;
She is abused, stol'n from me, and corrupted
By spells and medicines bought of mountebanks; For nature so
preposterously to err,
Being not deficient, blind, or lame of sense, Sans
witchcraft could not.

DUKE OF VENICE

Whoe'er he be that in this foul proceeding Hath thus
beguiled your daughter of herself And you of her, the
bloody book of law
You shall yourself read in the bitter letter
After your own sense, yea, though our proper son
Stood in your action.

BRABANTIO

Humbly I thank your grace.
Here is the man, this Moor, whom now, it seems, Your special
mandate for the state–affairs
Hath hither brought. **DUKE OF**

VENICE Senator

We are very sorry for't.

DUKE OF VENICE

[To OTHELLO] What, in your own part, can you say to this?

BRABANTIO

Nothing, but this is so.

OTHELLO

Most potent, grave, and reverend signiors, My very noble
and approved good masters, That I have ta'en away this old
man's daughter, It is most true; true, I have married her:
The very head and front of my offending
Hath this extent, no more. Rude am I in my speech, And little
bless'd with the soft phrase of peace:
For since these arms of mine had seven years' pith, Till now some
nine moons wasted, they have used Their dearest action in the
tented field,
And little of this great world can I speak, More than
pertains to feats of broil and battle, And therefore little
shall I grace my cause
In speaking for myself. Yet, by your gracious patience, I will a round
unvarnish'd tale deliver
Of my whole course of love; what drugs, what charms, What
conjuration and what mighty magic,
For such proceeding I am charged withal, I won his
daughter.

BRABANTIO

A maiden never bold;
Of spirit so still and quiet, that her motion Blush'd at
herself; and she, in spite of nature, Of years, of country,
credit, every thing,
To fall in love with what she fear'd to look on! It is a
judgment maim'd and most imperfect That will confess
perfection so could err Against all rules of nature, and must
be driven

To find out practises of cunning hell,
Why this should be. I therefore vouch again
That with some mixtures powerful o'er the blood, Or with
some dram conjured to this effect,
He wrought upon her.

DUKE OF VENICE

To vouch this, is no proof,
Without more wider and more overt test Than these thin
habits and poor likelihoods Of modern seeming do prefer
against him.

First Senator

But, Othello, speak:
Did you by indirect and forced courses
Subdue and poison this young maid's affections? Or came it
by request and such fair question
As soul to soul affordeth?

OTHELLO

I do beseech you,
Send for the lady to the Sagittary,
And let her speak of me before her father: If you do
find me foul in her report,
The trust, the office I do hold of you,
Not only take away, but let your sentence
Even fall upon my life.

DUKE OF VENICE

Fetch Desdemona hither.

OTHELLO

Ancient, conduct them: you best know the place.

[*Exeunt IAGO and Attendants*]

And, till she come, as truly as to heaven
I do confess the vices of my blood,
So justly to your grave ears I'll present How I did
thrive in this fair lady's love, And she in mine.

DUKE OF VENICE

Say it, Othello.

OTHELLO

Her father loved me; oft invited me; Still question'd
me the story of my life,
From year to year, the battles, sieges, fortunes, That I have
passed.
I ran it through, even from my boyish days, To the very
moment that he bade me tell it; Wherein I spake of most
disastrous chances, Of moving accidents by flood and
field
Of hair–breadth scapes i' the imminent deadly breach, Of being
taken by the insolent foe
And sold to slavery, of my redemption thence
And portance in my travels' history: Wherein of
antres vast and deserts idle,
Rough quarries, rocks and hills whose heads touch heaven
It was my hint to speak,—such was the process; And of the
Cannibals that each other eat,
The Anthropophagi and men whose heads
Do grow beneath their shoulders. This to hear

Would Desdemona seriously incline:
But still the house–affairs would draw her thence: Which ever
as she could with haste dispatch, She'ld come again, and with a
greedy ear

Devour up my discourse: which I observing, Took once a
pliant hour, and found good means To draw from her a prayer
of earnest heart
That I would all my pilgrimage dilate, Whereof by parcels
she had something heard, But not intentively: I did consent,
And often did beguile her of her tears,
When I did speak of some distressful stroke That my youth
suffer'd. My story being done, She gave me for my pains a
world of sighs:
She swore, in faith, twas strange, 'twas passing strange,
'Twas pitiful, 'twas wondrous pitiful:
She wish'd she had not heard it, yet she wish'd
That heaven had made her such a man: she thank'd me, And bade
me, if I had a friend that loved her,
I should but teach him how to tell my story.
And that would woo her. Upon this hint I spake: She loved
me for the dangers I had pass'd,
And I loved her that she did pity them. This only is
the witchcraft I have used: Here comes the lady; let
her witness it.

[*Enter DESDEMONA, IAGO, and Attendants*]

DUKE OF VENICE

I think this tale would win my daughter too. Good
Brabantio,
Take up this mangled matter at the best: Men do their
broken weapons rather use Than their bare hands.

BRABANTIO

I pray you, hear her speak:
If she confess that she was half the wooer, Destruction
on my head, if my bad blame

Light on the man! Come hither, gentle mistress: Do you
perceive in all this noble company Where most you owe
obedience?

DESDEMONA

My noble father,
I do perceive here a divided duty:
To you I am bound for life and education; My life and
education both do learn me
How to respect you; you are the lord of duty;
I am hitherto your daughter: but here's my husband, And so much
duty as my mother show'd
To you, preferring you before her father, So much I
challenge that I may profess Due to the Moor my lord.

BRABANTIO

God be wi' you! I have done.
Please it your grace, on to the state–affairs: I had rather
to adopt a child than get it. Come hither, Moor:
I here do give thee that with all my heart Which, but thou
hast already, with all my heart I would keep from thee. For
your sake, jewel,
I am glad at soul I have no other child: For thy escape
would teach me tyranny,
To hang clogs on them. I have done, my lord.

DUKE OF VENICE

Let me speak like yourself, and lay a sentence, Which, as a
grise or step, may help these lovers Into your favour.
When remedies are past, the griefs are ended

By seeing the worst, which late on hopes depended. To mourn a mischief that is past and gone
Is the next way to draw new mischief on. What cannot be preserved when fortune takes Patience her injury a mockery makes.
The robb'd that smiles steals something from the thief; He robs himself that spends a bootless grief.

BRABANTIO

So let the Turk of Cyprus us beguile; We lose it not, so long as we can smile.
He bears the sentence well that nothing bears
But the free comfort which from thence he hears, But he bears both the sentence and the sorrow That, to pay grief, must of poor patience borrow. These sentences, to sugar, or to gall, Being strong on both sides, are equivocal: But words are words; I never yet did hear
That the bruised heart was pierced through the ear.
I humbly beseech you, proceed to the affairs of state.

DUKE OF VENICE

The Turk with a most mighty preparation makes for Cyprus. Othello, the fortitude of the place is best known to you; and though we have there a substitute of most allowed sufficiency, yet opinion, a sovereign mistress of effects, throws a more safer voice on you: you must therefore be content to slubber the gloss of your new fortunes with this more stubborn and boisterous expedition.

OTHELLO

The tyrant custom, most grave senators, Hath made the flinty and steel couch of war My thrice–driven bed of down: I do agnise A natural and prompt alacrity

I find in hardness, and do undertake
These present wars against the Ottomites. Most humbly
therefore bending to your state, I crave fit disposition for
my wife.
Due reference of place and exhibition, With such
accommodation and besort As levels with her
breeding.

DUKE OF VENICE

If you please,
Be't at her father's.

BRABANTIO

I'll not have it so.

OTHELLO

Nor I.

DESDEMONA

Nor I; I would not there reside,
To put my father in impatient thoughts By being in his
eye. Most gracious duke, To my unfolding lend your
prosperous ear; And let me find a charter in your voice,
To assist my simpleness.

DUKE OF VENICE

What would You, Desdemona?

DESDEMONA

That I did love the Moor to live with him,
My downright violence and storm of fortunes
May trumpet to the world: my heart's subdued

Even to the very quality of my lord: I saw
Othello's visage in his mind,
And to his honour and his valiant parts Did I my soul
and fortunes consecrate. So that, dear lords, if I be left
behind,
A moth of peace, and he go to the war,
The rites for which I love him are bereft me, And I a
heavy interim shall support
By his dear absence. Let me go with him.

OTHELLO

Let her have your voices.
Vouch with me, heaven, I therefore beg it not, To please the
palate of my appetite,
Nor to comply with heat—the young affects
In me defunct—and proper satisfaction. But to be free
and bounteous to her mind:
And heaven defend your good souls, that you think
I will your serious and great business scant
For she is with me: no, when light–wing'd toys Of feather'd
Cupid seal with wanton dullness My speculative and officed
instruments,
That my disports corrupt and taint my business, Let
housewives make a skillet of my helm,
And all indign and base adversities
Make head against my estimation!

DUKE OF VENICE

Be it as you shall privately determine,
Either for her stay or going: the affair cries haste, And speed
must answer it.

First Senator

You must away to–night.

OTHELLO

With all my heart.

DUKE OF VENICE

At nine i' the morning here we'll meet again. Othello,
leave some officer behind,
And he shall our commission bring to you; With such
things else of quality and respect As doth import you.

OTHELLO

So please your grace, my ancient; A man he is
of honest and trust:
To his conveyance I assign my wife,
With what else needful your good grace shall think
To be sent after me.

DUKE OF VENICE

Let it be so.
Good night to every one.

To BRABANTIO

And, noble signior,
If virtue no delighted beauty lack,
Your son–in–law is far more fair than black.

First Senator

Adieu, brave Moor, use Desdemona well.

BRABANTIO

Look to her, Moor, if thou hast eyes to see: She has
deceived her father, and may thee.

[Exeunt DUKE OF VENICE, Senators, Officers, & c]

OTHELLO

My life upon her faith! Honest Iago, My
Desdemona must I leave to thee: I prithee, let thy
wife attend on her:
And bring them after in the best advantage. Come,
Desdemona: I have but an hour
Of love, of worldly matters and direction, To spend with
thee: we must obey the time.

[Exeunt OTHELLO and DESDEMONA]

RODERIGO

Iago,—

IAGO

What say'st thou, noble heart?

RODERIGO

What will I do, thinkest thou?

IAGO

Why, go to bed, and sleep.

RODERIGO

I will incontinently drown myself.

IAGO

If thou dost, I shall never love thee after. Why, thou silly gentleman!

RODERIGO

It is silliness to live when to live is torment; and then have we a prescription to die when death is our physician.

IAGO

O villainous! I have looked upon the world for four times seven years; and since I could distinguish betwixt a benefit and an injury, I never found man that knew how to love himself. Ere I would say, I would drown myself for the love of a guinea–hen,
I would change my humanity with a baboon.

RODERIGO

What should I do? I confess it is my shame to be so fond; but it is not in my virtue to amend it.

IAGO

Virtue! a fig! 'tis in ourselves that we are thus or thus. Our bodies are our gardens, to the which our wills are gardeners: so that if we will plant nettles, or sow lettuce, set hyssop and weed up thyme, supply it with one gender of herbs, or distract it with many, either to have it sterile with idleness, or manured with industry, why, the power and corrigible authority of this lies in our wills. If the balance of our lives had not one scale of reason to poise another of sensuality, the blood and baseness of our natures would conduct us to most preposterous conclusions: but we have reason to cool our raging motions, our carnal stings,
our unbitted lusts, whereof I take this that you call love to be a sect or scion.

RODERIGO

It cannot be.

IAGO

It is merely a lust of the blood and a permission of the will. Come, be a man. Drown thyself! drown cats and blind puppies. I have professed me thy friend and I confess me knit to thy

deserving with cables of perdurable toughness; I could never better stead
thee than now. Put money in thy purse; follow thou the wars; defeat thy
favour with an usurped beard; I say, put money in thy purse. It cannot be that
Desdemona should long continue her love to the Moor,— put money in thy
purse,—nor he his to her: it was a violent commencement, and thou shalt
see an answerable sequestration:—put but money in thy purse. These Moors
are changeable in their wills: fill thy purse with money:—the food that to
him now is as luscious as locusts, shall be to him shortly as bitter as
coloquintida. She must
change for youth: when she is sated with his body, she will find the error of
her choice: she must have change, she must: therefore put money in thy
purse. If thou wilt needs damn thyself, do it a more delicate way than
drowning. Make all the money thou canst: if sanctimony and a frail vow
betwixt an erring barbarian and a supersubtle Venetian not too hard for my
wits and all the tribe of hell, thou shalt enjoy her; therefore make money. A
pox of drowning thyself! it is clean out of the way: seek thou rather to be
hanged in compassing thy joy than to be drowned and go without her.

RODERIGO

Wilt thou be fast to my hopes, if I depend on the issue?

IAGO

Thou art sure of me:—go, make money:—I have told thee often, and I re–
tell thee again and again, I hate the Moor: my cause is hearted; thine hath no
less reason. Let us be conjunctive in our revenge against him: if thou canst
cuckold him, thou dost thyself a pleasure, me a sport. There are many
events in the womb of time which will be delivered. Traverse! go, provide
thy money. We will have more of this to–morrow. Adieu.

RODERIGO

Where shall we meet i' the morning?

IAGO

At my lodging.

RODERIGO

I'll be with thee betimes.

IAGO

Go to; farewell. Do you hear, Roderigo?

RODERIGO

What say you?

IAGO

No more of drowning, do you hear?

RODERIGO

I am changed: I'll go sell all my land. [*Exit*]

IAGO

Thus do I ever make my fool my purse:
For I mine own gain'd knowledge should profane, If I would
time expend with such a snipe.
But for my sport and profit. I hate the Moor: And it is
thought abroad, that 'twixt my sheets He has done my
office: I know not if't be true; But I, for mere suspicion in
that kind,
Will do as if for surety. He holds me well; The better
shall my purpose work on him.

Cassio's a proper man: let me see now: To get his
place and to plume up my will

In double knavery—How, how? Let's see:— After some time, to abuse Othello's ear
That he is too familiar with his wife. He hath a
person and a smooth dispose
To be suspected, framed to make women false. The Moor is of a free and open nature,
That thinks men honest that but seem to be so, And will as tenderly be led by the nose
As asses are.
I have't. It is engender'd. Hell and night
Must bring this monstrous birth to the world's light. [*Exit*]

ACT II

SCENE I

A Sea-port in Cyprus. an Open Place Near the Quay

[*Enter MONTANO and two Gentlemen*]

MONTANO

What from the cape can you discern at sea?

First Gentleman

Nothing at all: it is a highwrought flood; I cannot, 'twixt
the heaven and the main, Descry a sail.

MONTANO

Methinks the wind hath spoke aloud at land; A fuller blast
ne'er shook our battlements:
If it hath ruffian'd so upon the sea,
What ribs of oak, when mountains melt on them, Can hold the
mortise? What shall we hear of this?

Second Gentleman

A segregation of the Turkish fleet: For do but stand upon the foaming shore,
The chidden billow seems to pelt the clouds; The wind–shaked surge, with
high and monstrous mane, seems to cast water on the burning bear, And
quench the guards of the ever–fixed pole: I never did like molestation view
On the enchafed flood.

MONTANO

If that the Turkish fleet

Be not enshelter'd and embay'd, they are drown'd: It is impossible they bear it out.

[*Enter a third Gentleman*]

Third Gentleman

News, lads! our wars are done.
The desperate tempest hath so bang'd the Turks, That their designment halts: a noble ship of Venice Hath seen a grievous wreck and sufferance
On most part of their fleet.

MONTANO

How! is this true?

Third Gentleman

The ship is here put in,
A Veronesa; Michael Cassio,
Lieutenant to the warlike Moor Othello,
Is come on shore: the Moor himself at sea, And is in full commission here for Cyprus.

MONTANO

I am glad on't; 'tis a worthy governor.

Third Gentleman

But this same Cassio, though he speak of comfort Touching the Turkish loss, yet he looks sadly, And prays the Moor be safe; for they were parted With foul and violent tempest.

MONTANO

Pray heavens he be;

For I have served him, and the man commands
Like a full soldier. Let's to the seaside, ho! As well to
see the vessel that's come in
As to throw out our eyes for brave Othello, Even till we
make the main and the aerial blue An indistinct regard.

Third Gentleman

Come, let's do so:
For every minute is expectancy
Of more arrivance. [*Enter*

CASSIO] **CASSIO**

Thanks, you the valiant of this warlike isle, That so
approve the Moor! O, let the heavens Give him defence
against the elements,
For I have lost us him on a dangerous sea.

MONTANO

Is he well shipp'd?

CASSIO

His bark is stoutly timber'd, his pilot
Of very expert and approved allowance; Therefore my
hopes, not surfeited to death, Stand in bold cure.

A cry within 'A sail, a sail, a sail!' [Enter a

fourth Gentleman] **CASSIO**

What noise?

Fourth Gentleman

The town is empty; on the brow o' the sea
Stand ranks of people, and they cry 'A sail!'

CASSIO

My hopes do shape him for the governor.

Guns heard

Second Gentlemen

They do discharge their shot of courtesy: Our friends
at least.

CASSIO

I pray you, sir, go forth,
And give us truth who 'tis that is arrived.

Second Gentleman

I shall. [*Exit*]

MONTANO

But, good lieutenant, is your general wived?

CASSIO

Most fortunately: he hath achieved a maid That paragons
description and wild fame; One that excels the quirks of
blazoning pens, And in the essential vesture of creation
Does tire the ingener.

Re–enter second Gentleman

How now! who has put in?

Second Gentleman

'Tis one Iago, ancient to the general.

CASSIO

Has had most favourable and happy speed:
Tempests themselves, high seas, and howling winds, The gutter'd
rocks and congregated sands—
Traitors ensteep'd to clog the guiltless keel,— As having
sense of beauty, do omit
Their mortal natures, letting go safely by
The divine Desdemona.

MONTANO

What is she?

CASSIO

She that I spake of, our great captain's captain, Left in the
conduct of the bold Iago,
Whose footing here anticipates our thoughts
A se'nnight's speed. Great Jove, Othello guard, And swell his
sail with thine own powerful breath, That he may bless this bay
with his tall ship,
Make love's quick pants in Desdemona's arms, Give renew'd
fire to our extincted spirits
And bring all Cyprus comfort!

[*Enter DESDEMONA, EMILIA, IAGO, RODERIGO, and
Attendants*]

O, behold,

The riches of the ship is come on shore!
Ye men of Cyprus, let her have your knees. Hail to thee,
lady! and the grace of heaven, Before, behind thee, and
on every hand, Enwheel thee round!

DESDEMONA

I thank you, valiant Cassio.
What tidings can you tell me of my lord?

CASSIO

He is not yet arrived: nor know I aught
But that he's well and will be shortly here.

DESDEMONA

O, but I fear—How lost you company?

CASSIO

The great contention of the sea and skies
Parted our fellowship—But, hark! a sail.

Within 'A sail, a sail!' Guns heard

Second Gentleman

They give their greeting to the citadel; This likewise
is a friend.

CASSIO

See for the news. [*Exit

Gentleman*]

Good ancient, you are welcome.

To EMILIA

Welcome, mistress.
Let it not gall your patience, good Iago, That I extend my
manners; 'tis my breeding That gives me this bold show
of courtesy.

Kissing her

IAGO

Sir, would she give you so much of her lips As of her
tongue she oft bestows on me, You'll have enough.

DESDEMONA

Alas, she has no speech.

IAGO

In faith, too much;
I find it still, when I have list to sleep: Marry, before
your ladyship, I grant, She puts her tongue a little in
her heart, And chides with thinking.

EMILIA

You have little cause to say so.

IAGO

Come on, come on; you are pictures out of doors, Bells in your
parlors, wild–cats in your kitchens, Saints m your injuries,
devils being offended,
Players in your housewifery, and housewives' in your beds.

DESDEMONA

O, fie upon thee, slanderer!

IAGO

Nay, it is true, or else I am a Turk:
You rise to play and go to bed to work.

EMILIA

You shall not write my praise.

IAGO

No, let me not.

DESDEMONA

What wouldst thou write of me, if thou shouldst praise me?

IAGO

O gentle lady, do not put me to't; For I am
nothing, if not critical.

DESDEMONA

Come on assay. There's one gone to the harbour?

IAGO

Ay, madam.

DESDEMONA

I am not merry; but I do beguile
The thing I am, by seeming otherwise. Come, how
wouldst thou praise me?

IAGO

I am about it; but indeed my invention
Comes from my pate as birdlime does from frize; It plucks out
brains and all: but my Muse labours, And thus she is deliver'd.
If she be fair and wise, fairness and wit, The one's for
use, the other useth it.

DESDEMONA

Well praised! How if she be black and witty?

IAGO

If she be black, and thereto have a wit,
She'll find a white that shall her blackness fit.

DESDEMONA

Worse and worse.

EMILIA

How if fair and foolish?

IAGO

She never yet was foolish that was fair; For even her
folly help'd her to an heir.

DESDEMONA

These are old fond paradoxes to make fools laugh i' the alehouse. What
miserable praise hast thou for her that's foul and foolish?

IAGO

There's none so foul and foolish thereunto,

But does foul pranks which fair and wise ones do.

DESDEMONA

O heavy ignorance! thou praisest the worst best. But what praise couldst thou bestow on a deserving woman indeed, one that, in the authority of her merit, did justly put on the vouch of very malice itself?

IAGO

She that was ever fair and never proud, Had tongue at will
and yet was never loud, Never lack'd gold and yet went
never gay, Fled from her wish and yet said 'Now I may,'
She that being anger'd, her revenge being nigh, Bade her
wrong stay and her displeasure fly, She that in wisdom never
was so frail
To change the cod's head for the salmon's tail; She that could
think and ne'er disclose her mind, See suitors following and
not look behind,
She was a wight, if ever such wight were,—

DESDEMONA

To do what?

IAGO

To suckle fools and chronicle small beer.

DESDEMONA

O most lame and impotent conclusion! Do not learn of him, Emilia, though he be thy husband. How say you, Cassio? is he not a most profane and liberal counsellor?

CASSIO

He speaks home, madam: You may relish him more in the soldier than in the scholar.

IAGO

[Aside] He takes her by the palm: ay, well said, whisper: with as little a web as this will I ensnare as great a fly as Cassio. Ay, smile upon her, do; I will gyve thee in thine own courtship. You say true; 'tis so, indeed: if such tricks as these strip you out of your lieutenantry, it had been better you had not kissed your three fingers so oft, which now again you are most apt to play the sir in. Very good; well kissed! an excellent courtesy! 'tis so, indeed. Yet again your fingers to your lips? would they were clyster–pipes for your sake!

Trumpet within

The Moor! I know his trumpet.

CASSIO

'Tis truly so.

DESDEMONA

Let's meet him and receive him.

CASSIO

Lo, where he comes!

[*Enter OTHELLO and Attendants*]

OTHELLO

O my fair warrior!

DESDEMONA

My dear Othello!

OTHELLO

It gives me wonder great as my content
To see you here before me. O my soul's joy! If after every
tempest come such calms,
May the winds blow till they have waken'd death! And let the
labouring bark climb hills of seas Olympus–high and duck
again as low
As hell's from heaven! If it were now to die,
'Twere now to be most happy; for, I fear, My soul hath
her content so absolute
That not another comfort like to this
Succeeds in unknown fate.

DESDEMONA

The heavens forbid
But that our loves and comforts should increase, Even as our
days do grow!

OTHELLO

Amen to that, sweet powers!
I cannot speak enough of this content; It stops me
here; it is too much of joy:
And this, and this, the greatest discords be

Kissing her

That e'er our hearts shall make!

IAGO

[Aside] O, you are well tuned now!
But I'll set down the pegs that make this music, As honest as
I am.

OTHELLO

Come, let us to the castle. News, friends; our wars are done, the Turks are drown'd. How does my old acquaintance of this isle? Honey, you shall be well desired in Cyprus; I have found great love amongst them. O my sweet, I prattle out of fashion, and I dote In mine own comforts. I prithee, good Iago, Go to the bay and disembark my coffers: Bring thou the master to the citadel; He is a good one, and his worthiness Does challenge much respect. Come, Desdemona, Once more, well met at Cyprus.

[Exeunt OTHELLO, DESDEMONA, and Attendants]

IAGO

Do thou meet me presently at the harbour. Come hither. If thou be'st valiant,— as, they say, base men being in love have then a nobility in their natures more than is native to them—list me. The lieutenant tonight watches on the court of guard:—first, I must tell thee this—Desdemona is directly in love with him.

RODERIGO

With him! why, 'tis not possible.

IAGO

Lay thy finger thus, and let thy soul be instructed. Mark me with what violence she first loved the Moor, but for bragging and telling her fantastical lies: and will she love him still for prating? let not thy discreet heart think it. Her eye must be fed; and what delight shall she have to look on the devil? When the blood is made dull with the act of sport, there should be, again to inflame it and to give satiety a fresh appetite, loveliness in favour, sympathy in years, manners and beauties; all which the Moor is defective in: now, for want of these required conveniences, her delicate tenderness will find itself abused, begin to heave the gorge, disrelish and abhor the Moor; very nature will instruct her in it and compel her to some second choice. Now, sir, this granted,—as it is a most pregnant and unforced position—who stands so eminent in the degree of this fortune as Cassio does? a knave very voluble; no further conscionable than in putting on the mere form of civil and humane seeming, for the better compassing of his salt and most hidden loose affection? why, none; why, none: a slipper and subtle knave, a finder of occasions, that has an eye can stamp and counterfeit advantages, though true advantage never present itself; a devilish knave. Besides, the knave is handsome, young, and hath all those requisites in him that folly and green minds look after: a pestilent complete knave; and the woman hath found him already.

RODERIGO

I cannot believe that in her; she's full of most blessed condition.

IAGO

Blessed fig's–end! the wine she drinks is made of grapes: if she had been blessed, she would never have loved the Moor. Blessed pudding! Didst thou not see her paddle with the palm of his hand? didst not mark that?

RODERIGO

Yes, that I did; but that was but courtesy.

IAGO

Lechery, by this hand; an index and obscure prologue to the history of lust and foul thoughts. They met so near with their lips that their breaths embraced together. Villanous thoughts, Roderigo! when these mutualities so marshal the way, hard at hand comes the master and main exercise, the incorporate conclusion, Pish! But, sir, be you ruled by me: I have brought you from Venice. Watch you to–night; for the command, I'll lay't upon you. Cassio knows you not. I'll not be far from you: do you find some occasion to anger Cassio, either by speaking too loud, or tainting his discipline; or from what other course you please, which the time shall more favourably minister.

RODERIGO

Well.

IAGO

Sir, he is rash and very sudden in choler, and haply may strike at you: provoke him, that he may; for even out of that will I cause these of Cyprus to mutiny; whose qualification shall come into no true taste again but by the displanting of Cassio. So shall you have a shorter journey to your desires by the means I shall then have to prefer them; and the impediment most profitably removed, without the which there were no expectation of our prosperity.

RODERIGO

I will do this, if I can bring it to any opportunity.

IAGO

I warrant thee. Meet me by and by at the citadel: I must fetch his necessaries ashore. Farewell.

RODERIGO

Adieu. [*Exit*] **IAGO**

That Cassio loves her, I do well believe it; That she loves him, 'tis apt and of great credit: The Moor, howbeit that I endure him not,
Is of a constant, loving, noble nature,
And I dare think he'll prove to Desdemona
A most dear husband. Now, I do love her too; Not out of absolute lust, though peradventure
I stand accountant for as great a sin, But partly
led to diet my revenge,

For that I do suspect the lusty Moor
Hath leap'd into my seat; the thought whereof Doth, like a
poisonous mineral, gnaw my inwards; And nothing can or shall
content my soul
Till I am even'd with him, wife for wife, Or failing so,
yet that I put the Moor
At least into a jealousy so strong
That judgment cannot cure. Which thing to do, If this poor
trash of Venice, whom I trash
For his quick hunting, stand the putting on, I'll have our
Michael Cassio on the hip, Abuse him to the Moor in the
rank garb— For I fear Cassio with my night–cap too—
Make the Moor thank me, love me and reward me. For making
him egregiously an ass
And practising upon his peace and quiet
Even to madness. 'Tis here, but yet confused: Knavery's
plain face is never seen tin used.

[*Exit*]

SCENE II

A Street

[*Enter a Herald with a proclamation; People following*]

Herald

It is Othello's pleasure, our noble and valiant general, that, upon certain
tidings now arrived, importing the mere perdition of the Turkish fleet, every
man put himself into triumph; some to dance, some to make bonfires, each
man to what sport and revels his addiction leads him: for, besides these
beneficial news, it is the celebration of his nuptial. So much was his pleasure
should be proclaimed. All offices are open, and there
is full liberty of feasting from this present hour of five till the bell have told
eleven. Heaven bless the isle of Cyprus and our noble general Othello!

[*Exeunt*]

Scene III

A Hall in the Castle

[*Enter OTHELLO, DESDEMONA, CASSIO, and Attendants*]

OTHELLO

> Good Michael, look you to the guard to–night: Let's teach
> ourselves that honourable stop,
> Not to outsport discretion.

CASSIO

> Iago hath direction what to do;
> But, notwithstanding, with my personal eye
> Will I look to't.

OTHELLO

> Iago is most honest.
> Michael, good night: to–morrow with your earliest
> Let me have speech with you.

To DESDEMONA

> Come, my dear love,
> The purchase made, the fruits are to ensue; That profit's
> yet to come 'tween me and you. Good night.

[*Exeunt OTHELLO, DESDEMONA, and Attendants*] [*Enter

IAGO*]

CASSIO

Welcome, Iago; we must to the watch.

IAGO

Not this hour, lieutenant; 'tis not yet ten o' the clock. Our general cast us thus early for the love of his Desdemona; who let us not therefore blame: he hath not yet made wanton the night with her; and she is sport for Jove.

CASSIO

She's a most exquisite lady.

IAGO

And, I'll warrant her, fun of game.

CASSIO

Indeed, she's a most fresh and delicate creature.

IAGO

What an eye she has! methinks it sounds a parley of provocation.

CASSIO

An inviting eye; and yet methinks right modest.

IAGO

And when she speaks, is it not an alarum to love?

CASSIO

She is indeed perfection.

IAGO

Well, happiness to their sheets! Come, lieutenant, I have a stoup of wine; and here without are a brace of Cyprus gallants that would fain have a measure to the health of black Othello.

CASSIO

Not to–night, good Iago: I have very poor and unhappy brains for drinking: I could well wish courtesy would invent some other custom of entertainment.

IAGO

O, they are our friends; but one cup: I'll drink for you.

CASSIO

I have drunk but one cup to–night, and that was craftily qualified too, and, behold, what innovation it makes here: I am unfortunate in the infirmity, and dare not task my weakness with any more.

IAGO

What, man! 'tis a night of revels: the gallants desire it.

CASSIO

Where are they?

IAGO

Here at the door; I pray you, call them in.

CASSIO

I'll do't; but it dislikes me. [*Exit*]

IAGO

If I can fasten but one cup upon him,
With that which he hath drunk to–night already, He'll be as
full of quarrel and offence
As my young mistress' dog. Now, my sick fool Roderigo, Whom love
hath turn'd almost the wrong side out,
To Desdemona hath to–night caroused Potations pottle–
deep; and he's to watch: Three lads of Cyprus, noble
swelling spirits, That hold their honours in a wary
distance, The very elements of this warlike isle,
Have I to–night fluster'd with flowing cups, And they watch
too. Now, 'mongst this flock of drunkards,
Am I to put our Cassio in some action
That may offend the isle.—But here they come: If
consequence do but approve my dream,
My boat sails freely, both with wind and stream.

*Re–enter CASSIO; with him MONTANO and Gentlemen; servants following
with wine*

CASSIO

'Fore God, they have given me a rouse already.

MONTANO

Good faith, a little one; not past a pint, as I am a soldier.

IAGO

Some wine, ho!

Sings

> And let me the canakin clink, clink; And let me
> the canakin clink
> A soldier's a man;

A life's but a span;
Why, then, let a soldier drink. Some wine,
boys!

CASSIO

'Fore God, an excellent song.

IAGO

I learned it in England, where, indeed, they are most potent in potting: your
Dane, your German, and your swag–bellied Hollander—Drink, ho!—are
nothing to your English.

CASSIO

Is your Englishman so expert in his drinking?

IAGO

Why, he drinks you, with facility, your Dane dead drunk; he sweats not to
overthrow your Almain; he gives your Hollander a vomit, ere the next pottle
can be filled.

CASSIO

To the health of our general!

MONTANO

I am for it, lieutenant; and I'll do you justice.

IAGO

O sweet England!
King Stephen was a worthy peer, His breeches
cost him but a crown; He held them sixpence all
too dear, With that he call'd the tailor lown. He
was a wight of high renown,

And thou art but of low degree:
'Tis pride that pulls the country down; Then take
thine auld cloak about thee. Some wine, ho!

CASSIO

Why, this is a more exquisite song than the other.

IAGO

Will you hear't again?

CASSIO

No; for I hold him to be unworthy of his place that does those things. Well, God's above all; and there be souls must be saved, and there be souls must not be saved.

IAGO

It's true, good lieutenant.

CASSIO

For mine own part,—no offence to the general, nor any man of quality,—I hope to be saved.

IAGO

And so do I too, lieutenant.

CASSIO

Ay, but, by your leave, not before me; the lieutenant is to be saved before the ancient. Let's have no more of this; let's to our affairs.—Forgive us our sins!—Gentlemen, let's look to our business. Do not think, gentlemen. I am drunk: this is my ancient; this is my right hand, and this is my left: I am not drunk now; I can stand well enough, and speak well enough.

All

Excellent well.

CASSIO

Why, very well then; you must not think then that I am drunk. [*Exit*]

MONTANO

To the platform, masters; come, let's set the watch.

IAGO

You see this fellow that is gone before; He is a
soldier fit to stand by Caesar
And give direction: and do but see his vice;
'Tis to his virtue a just equinox,
The one as long as the other: 'tis pity of him. I fear the
trust Othello puts him in.
On some odd time of his infirmity, Will shake
this island.

MONTANO

But is he often thus?

IAGO

'Tis evermore the prologue to his sleep: He'll watch
the horologe a double set,
If drink rock not his cradle.

MONTANO

It were well
The general were put in mind of it.

Perhaps he sees it not; or his good nature Prizes the
virtue that appears in Cassio, And looks not on his evils:
is not this true?

[*Enter RODERIGO*]

IAGO

[Aside to him] How now, Roderigo! I pray you,
after the lieutenant; go.

[*Exit RODERIGO*]

MONTANO

And 'tis great pity that the noble Moor
Should hazard such a place as his own second
With one of an ingraft infirmity: It were an
honest action to say So to the Moor.

IAGO

Not I, for this fair island:
I do love Cassio well; and would do much
To cure him of this evil—But, hark! what noise?

Cry within: 'Help! help!'

Re–enter CASSIO, driving in RODERIGO

CASSIO

You rogue! you rascal!

MONTANO

What's the matter, lieutenant?

CASSIO

> A knave teach me my duty!
> I'll beat the knave into a twiggen bottle.

RODERIGO

> Beat me!

CASSIO

> Dost thou prate, rogue? *Striking*

RODERIGO **MONTANO**

> Nay, good lieutenant;

Staying him

> I pray you, sir, hold your hand.

CASSIO

> Let me go, sir,
> Or I'll knock you o'er the mazzard.

MONTANO

> Come, come, you're drunk.

> **CASSIO** Drunk! *They*

> > *fight*

IAGO

> [Aside to RODERIGO] Away, I say; go out, and cry a mutiny.

[Exit RODERIGO]

Nay, good lieutenant,—alas, gentlemen;— Help, ho!—
Lieutenant,—sir,—Montano,—sir; Help, masters!—Here's a
goodly watch indeed!

Bell rings

Who's that which rings the bell?—Diablo, ho! The town will
rise: God's will, lieutenant, hold! You will be shamed for
ever.

Re–enter OTHELLO and Attendants

OTHELLO

What is the matter here?

MONTANO

'Zounds, I bleed still; I am hurt to the death.

Faints

OTHELLO

Hold, for your lives!

IAGO

Hold, ho! Lieutenant,—sir—Montano,—gentlemen,— Have you
forgot all sense of place and duty?
Hold! the general speaks to you; hold, hold, for shame!

OTHELLO

Why, how now, ho! from whence ariseth this? Are we
turn'd Turks, and to ourselves do that Which heaven hath
forbid the Ottomites?

For Christian shame, put by this barbarous brawl: He that stirs
next to carve for his own rage
Holds his soul light; he dies upon his motion. Silence that
dreadful bell: it frights the isle
From her propriety. What is the matter, masters? Honest Iago,
that look'st dead with grieving, Speak, who began this? on thy
love, I charge thee.

IAGO

I do not know: friends all but now, even now, In quarter,
and in terms like bride and groom Devesting them for bed;
and then, but now— As if some planet had unwitted men—
Swords out, and tilting one at other's breast,
In opposition bloody. I cannot speak Any beginning
to this peevish odds; And would in action glorious I
had lost
Those legs that brought me to a part of it!

OTHELLO

How comes it, Michael, you are thus forgot?

CASSIO

I pray you, pardon me; I cannot speak.

OTHELLO

Worthy Montano, you were wont be civil; The gravity
and stillness of your youth
The world hath noted, and your name is great In mouths of
wisest censure: what's the matter, That you unlace your
reputation thus
And spend your rich opinion for the name
Of a night–brawler? give me answer to it.

MONTANO

Worthy Othello, I am hurt to danger: Your officer, Iago, can inform you,—
While I spare speech, which something now offends me,— Of all that I do
know: nor know I aught By me that's said or done amiss this night; Unless
self–charity be sometimes a vice, And to defend ourselves it be a sin When
violence assails us.

OTHELLO

Now, by heaven,
My blood begins my safer guides to rule;
And passion, having my best judgment collied, Assays to
lead the way: if I once stir,
Or do but lift this arm, the best of you Shall sink in my
rebuke. Give me to know How this foul rout began,
who set it on; And he that is approved in this offence,
Though he had twinn'd with me, both at a birth, Shall lose
me. What! in a town of war,
Yet wild, the people's hearts brimful of fear, To manage
private and domestic quarrel,
In night, and on the court and guard of safety!
'Tis monstrous. Iago, who began't?

MONTANO

If partially affined, or leagued in office, Thou dost
deliver more or less than truth, Thou art no soldier.

IAGO

Touch me not so near:
I had rather have this tongue cut from my mouth Than it
should do offence to Michael Cassio; Yet, I persuade myself,
to speak the truth

Shall nothing wrong him. Thus it is, general. Montano and
myself being in speech,
There comes a fellow crying out for help:
And Cassio following him with determined sword, To execute
upon him. Sir, this gentleman
Steps in to Cassio, and entreats his pause: Myself the
crying fellow did pursue,
Lest by his clamour—as it so fell out—
The town might fall in fright: he, swift of foot, Outran my
purpose; and I return'd the rather For that I heard the clink
and fall of swords, And Cassio high in oath; which till to–
night
I ne'er might say before. When I came back— For this was
brief—I found them close together, At blow and thrust; even
as again they were When you yourself did part them.
More of this matter cannot I report:
But men are men; the best sometimes forget: Though
Cassio did some little wrong to him,
As men in rage strike those that wish them best, Yet surely
Cassio, I believe, received
From him that fled some strange indignity, Which
patience could not pass.

OTHELLO

I know, Iago,
Thy honesty and love doth mince this matter, Making it light
to Cassio. Cassio, I love thee But never more be officer of
mine.

Re–enter DESDEMONA, attended

Look, if my gentle love be not raised up! I'll make thee
an example.

DESDEMONA

What's the matter?

OTHELLO

All's well now, sweeting; come away to bed.
Sir, for your hurts, myself will be your surgeon: Lead him
off.

To MONTANO, who is led off

Iago, look with care about the town,
And silence those whom this vile brawl distracted. Come,
Desdemona: 'tis the soldiers' life
To have their balmy slumbers waked with strife. [*Exeunt all*

but IAGO and CASSIO]

IAGO

What, are you hurt, lieutenant?

CASSIO

Ay, past all surgery.

IAGO

Marry, heaven forbid!

CASSIO

Reputation, reputation, reputation! O, I have lost my reputation! I have lost
the immortal part of myself, and what remains is bestial. My reputation, Iago,
my reputation!

IAGO

As I am an honest man, I thought you had received some bodily wound; there
is more sense in that than in reputation.
Reputation is an idle and most false imposition: oft got without

merit, and lost without deserving: you have lost no reputation at all, unless you repute yourself such a loser. What, man! there
are ways to recover the general again: you are but now cast in his mood, a punishment more in policy than in malice, even so as one would beat his offenceless dog to affright an imperious lion: sue to him again, and he's yours.

CASSIO

I will rather sue to be despised than to deceive so good a commander with so slight, so drunken, and so indiscreet an officer. Drunk? and speak parrot? and squabble? swagger? swear? and discourse fustian with one's own shadow? O thou invisible spirit of wine, if thou hast no name to be known by, let us call thee devil!

IAGO

What was he that you followed with your sword? What had he done to you?

CASSIO

I know not.

IAGO

Is't possible?

CASSIO

I remember a mass of things, but nothing distinctly; a quarrel, but nothing wherefore. O God, that men should put an enemy in their mouths to steal away their brains! that we should, with
joy, pleasance revel and applause, transform ourselves into beasts!

IAGO

Why, but you are now well enough: how came you thus

recovered?

CASSIO

It hath pleased the devil drunkenness to give place to the devil wrath; one unperfectness shows me another, to make me frankly despise myself.

IAGO

Come, you are too severe a moraler: as the time, the place, and the condition of this country stands, I could heartily wish this had not befallen; but, since it is as it is, mend it for your own good.

CASSIO

I will ask him for my place again; he shall tell me I am a drunkard! Had I as many mouths as Hydra, such an answer would stop them all. To be now a sensible man, by and by a fool, and presently a beast! O strange! Every inordinate cup is unblessed and the ingredient is a devil.

IAGO

Come, come, good wine is a good familiar creature, if it be well used: exclaim no more against it. And, good lieutenant, I think you think I love you.

CASSIO

I have well approved it, sir. I drunk!

IAGO

You or any man living may be drunk! at a time, man. I'll tell you what you shall do. Our general's wife is now the general: may say so in this respect, for that he hath devoted and given up himself to the contemplation, mark, and denotement of her parts and graces: confess yourself freely to her; importune her help to

put you in your place again: she is of so free, so kind, so apt, so blessed a disposition, she holds it a vice in her goodness not to do more than she is requested: this broken joint between you
and her husband entreat her to splinter; and, my fortunes against any lay worth naming, this crack of your love shall grow stronger than it was before.

CASSIO

You advise me well.

IAGO

I protest, in the sincerity of love and honest kindness.

CASSIO

I think it freely; and betimes in the morning I will beseech the virtuous Desdemona to undertake for me: I am desperate of my fortunes if they cheque me here.

IAGO

You are in the right. Good night, lieutenant; I must to the watch.
CASSIO: Good night, honest Iago.

[*Exit*]

IAGO

And what's he then that says I play the villain? When this
advice is free I give and honest, Probal to thinking and
indeed the course
To win the Moor again? For 'tis most easy
The inclining Desdemona to subdue
In any honest suit: she's framed as fruitful
As the free elements. And then for her
To win the Moor—were't to renounce his baptism, All seals and
symbols of redeemed sin,

His soul is so enfetter'd to her love,
That she may make, unmake, do what she list, Even as her
appetite shall play the god
With his weak function. How am I then a villain To counsel
Cassio to this parallel course, Directly to his good? Divinity
of hell!
When devils will the blackest sins put on, They do suggest
at first with heavenly shows, As I do now: for whiles this
honest fool
Plies Desdemona to repair his fortunes
And she for him pleads strongly to the Moor, I'll pour this
pestilence into his ear,
That she repeals him for her body's lust;
And by how much she strives to do him good, She shall
undo her credit with the Moor.
So will I turn her virtue into pitch,
And out of her own goodness make the net
That shall enmesh them all.

Re–enter RODERIGO

How now, Roderigo!

RODERIGO

I do follow here in the chase, not like a hound that hunts, but one that fills up
the cry. My money is almost spent; I have been to–night exceedingly well
cudgelled; and I think the issue will be, I shall have so much experience for
my pains, and so, with no money at all and a little more wit, return again to
Venice.

IAGO

How poor are they that have not patience! What wound
did ever heal but by degrees?
Thou know'st we work by wit, and not by witchcraft; And wit
depends on dilatory time.
Does't not go well? Cassio hath beaten thee.

And thou, by that small hurt, hast cashier'd Cassio: Though other things grow fair against the sun,
Yet fruits that blossom first will first be ripe: Content thyself awhile. By the mass, 'tis morning; Pleasure and action make the hours seem short. Retire thee; go where thou art billeted: Away, I say; thou shalt know more hereafter: Nay, get thee gone.

[*Exit RODERIGO*]

Two things are to be done:
My wife must move for Cassio to her mistress; I'll set her on;
Myself the while to draw the Moor apart,
And bring him jump when he may Cassio find
Soliciting his wife: ay, that's the way
Dull not device by coldness and delay. [*Exit*]

ACT III

Scene I

Before the Castle

[Enter CASSIO and some Musicians]

CASSIO

Masters, play here; I will content your pains;
Something that's brief; and bid 'Good morrow, general.'

Music

[Enter Clown]

Clown

Why masters, have your instruments been in Naples, that they speak i' the
nose thus?

First Musician

How, sir, how!

Clown

Are these, I pray you, wind–instruments?

First Musician

Ay, marry, are they, sir.

Clown

O, thereby hangs a tail.

First Musician

Whereby hangs a tale, sir?

Clown

Marry. sir, by many a wind–instrument that I know. But, masters, here's money for you: and the general so likes your music, that he desires you, for love's sake, to make no more noise with it.

First Musician

Well, sir, we will not.

Clown

If you have any music that may not be heard, to't again: but, as they say to hear music the general does not greatly care.

First Musician

We have none such, sir.

Clown

Then put up your pipes in your bag, for I'll away: go; vanish into air; away!

[*Exeunt Musicians*]

CASSIO

Dost thou hear, my honest friend?

Clown

No, I hear not your honest friend; I hear you.

CASSIO

Prithee, keep up thy quillets. There's a poor piece of gold for thee: if the gentlewoman that attends the general's wife be stirring, tell her there's one Cassio entreats her a little favour of speech: wilt thou do this?

Clown

She is stirring, sir: if she will stir hither, I shall seem to notify unto her.

CASSIO

Do, good my friend. [*Exit Clown*]

[*Enter IAGO*] In happy time, Iago.

IAGO

You have not been a–bed, then?

CASSIO

Why, no; the day had broke
Before we parted. I have made bold, Iago, To send in to
your wife: my suit to her
Is, that she will to virtuous Desdemona
Procure me some access.

IAGO

I'll send her to you presently;
And I'll devise a mean to draw the Moor
Out of the way, that your converse and business
May be more free.

CASSIO

I humbly thank you for't. [*Exit IAGO*]

I never knew
A Florentine more kind and honest. [*Enter*

EMILIA]

EMILIA

Good morrow, good Lieutenant: I am sorry For your
displeasure; but all will sure be well. The general and his
wife are talking of it;
And she speaks for you stoutly: the Moor replies, That he you
hurt is of great fame in Cyprus,
And great affinity, and that in wholesome wisdom
He might not but refuse you; but he protests he loves you
And needs no other suitor but his likings To take the
safest occasion by the front To bring you in again.

CASSIO

Yet, I beseech you,
If you think fit, or that it may be done,
Give me advantage of some brief discourse
With Desdemona alone.

EMILIA

Pray you, come in;
I will bestow you where you shall have time
To speak your bosom freely.

CASSIO

I am much bound to you. [*Exeunt*]

Scene II

A Room in the Castle

[*Enter OTHELLO, IAGO, and Gentlemen*]

OTHELLO

These letters give, Iago, to the pilot; And by him do my duties to the senate: That done, I will be walking on the works; Repair there to me.

IAGO

Well, my good lord, I'll do't.

OTHELLO

This fortification, gentlemen, shall we see't?

Gentleman

We'll wait upon your lordship. [*Exeunt*]

Scene III

The Garden of the Castle

[*Enter DESDEMONA, CASSIO, and EMILIA*]

DESDEMONA

Be thou assured, good Cassio, I will do
All my abilities in thy behalf.

EMILIA

Good madam, do: I warrant it grieves my husband, As if the case
were his.

DESDEMONA

O, that's an honest fellow. Do not doubt, Cassio, But I will
have my lord and you again
As friendly as you were.

CASSIO

Bounteous madam,
Whatever shall become of Michael Cassio, He's never
any thing but your true servant.

DESDEMONA

I know't; I thank you. You do love my lord:
You have known him long; and be you well assured
He shall in strangeness stand no further off
Than in a polite distance.

CASSIO

Ay, but, lady,
That policy may either last so long,
Or feed upon such nice and waterish diet, Or breed
itself so out of circumstance,
That, I being absent and my place supplied, My general
will forget my love and service.

DESDEMONA

Do not doubt that; before Emilia here
I give thee warrant of thy place: assure thee, If I do vow a
friendship, I'll perform it
To the last article: my lord shall never rest;
I'll watch him tame and talk him out of patience; His bed shall
seem a school, his board a shrift; I'll intermingle every thing
he does
With Cassio's suit: therefore be merry, Cassio; For thy
solicitor shall rather die
Than give thy cause away.

EMILIA

Madam, here comes my lord.

CASSIO

Madam, I'll take my leave.

DESDEMONA

Why, stay, and hear me speak.

CASSIO

Madam, not now: I am very ill at ease, Unfit for
mine own purposes.

DESDEMONA

Well, do your discretion. [*Exit

CASSIO]

[*Enter OTHELLO and IAGO*]

IAGO

Ha! I like not that.

OTHELLO

What dost thou say?

IAGO

Nothing, my lord: or if—I know not what.

OTHELLO

Was not that Cassio parted from my wife?

IAGO

Cassio, my lord! No, sure, I cannot think it, That he
would steal away so guilty–like, Seeing you coming.

OTHELLO

I do believe 'twas he.

DESDEMONA

How now, my lord!
I have been talking with a suitor here,
A man that languishes in your displeasure.

OTHELLO

Who is't you mean?

DESDEMONA

Why, your lieutenant, Cassio. Good my lord, If I have any
grace or power to move you, His present reconciliation
take;
For if he be not one that truly loves you, That errs in
ignorance and not in cunning, I have no judgment in an
honest face:
I prithee, call him back.

OTHELLO

Went he hence now?

DESDEMONA

Ay, sooth; so humbled
That he hath left part of his grief with me,
To suffer with him. Good love, call him back.

OTHELLO

Not now, sweet Desdemona; some other time.

DESDEMONA

But shall't be shortly?

OTHELLO

The sooner, sweet, for you.

DESDEMONA

Shall't be to–night at supper?

OTHELLO

No, not to–night.

DESDEMONA

To–morrow dinner, then?

OTHELLO

I shall not dine at home;
I meet the captains at the citadel.

DESDEMONA

Why, then, to–morrow night; or Tuesday morn; On Tuesday
noon, or night; on Wednesday morn: I prithee, name the time,
but let it not
Exceed three days: in faith, he's penitent;
And yet his trespass, in our common reason— Save that, they
say, the wars must make examples Out of their best—is not
almost a fault
To incur a private cheque. When shall he come? Tell me,
Othello: I wonder in my soul,
What you would ask me, that I should deny,
Or stand so mammering on. What! Michael Cassio, That came a–
wooing with you, and so many a time, When I have spoke of you
dispraisingly,
Hath ta'en your part; to have so much to do
To bring him in! Trust me, I could do much,—

OTHELLO

Prithee, no more: let him come when he will; I will deny
thee nothing.

DESDEMONA

Why, this is not a boon;
'Tis as I should entreat you wear your gloves,
Or feed on nourishing dishes, or keep you warm, Or sue to you
to do a peculiar profit
To your own person: nay, when I have a suit
Wherein I mean to touch your love indeed, It shall be full
of poise and difficult weight And fearful to be granted.

OTHELLO

I will deny thee nothing:
Whereon, I do beseech thee, grant me this, To leave me
but a little to myself.

DESDEMONA

Shall I deny you? no: farewell, my lord.

OTHELLO

Farewell, my Desdemona: I'll come to thee straight.

DESDEMONA

Emilia, come. Be as your fancies teach you; Whate'er you
be, I am obedient.

[*Exeunt DESDEMONA and EMILIA*]

OTHELLO

Excellent wretch! Perdition catch my soul, But I do love
thee! and when I love thee not, Chaos is come again.

IAGO

My noble lord—

OTHELLO

What dost thou say, Iago?

IAGO

Did Michael Cassio, when you woo'd my lady, Know of your love?

OTHELLO

He did, from first to last: why dost thou ask?

IAGO

But for a satisfaction of my thought; No further harm.

OTHELLO

Why of thy thought, Iago?

IAGO

I did not think he had been acquainted with her.

OTHELLO

O, yes; and went between us very oft.

IAGO

Indeed!

OTHELLO

Indeed! ay, indeed: discern'st thou aught in that? Is he not honest?

IAGO

Honest, my lord!

OTHELLO

Honest! ay, honest.

IAGO

My lord, for aught I know.

OTHELLO

What dost thou think?

IAGO

Think, my lord!

OTHELLO

Think, my lord!
By heaven, he echoes me,
As if there were some monster in his thought
Too hideous to be shown. Thou dost mean something: I heard thee
say even now, thou likedst not that,
When Cassio left my wife: what didst not like? And when I
told thee he was of my counsel
In my whole course of wooing, thou criedst 'Indeed!' And didst
contract and purse thy brow together,
As if thou then hadst shut up in thy brain Some horrible
conceit: if thou dost love me, Show me thy thought.

IAGO

My lord, you know I love you.

OTHELLO

I think thou dost;
And, for I know thou'rt full of love and honesty,
And weigh'st thy words before thou givest them breath, Therefore
these stops of thine fright me the more:
For such things in a false disloyal knave
Are tricks of custom, but in a man that's just They are close
delations, working from the heart That passion cannot rule.

IAGO

For Michael Cassio,
I dare be sworn I think that he is honest.

OTHELLO

I think so too.

IAGO

Men should be what they seem;
Or those that be not, would they might seem none!

OTHELLO

Certain, men should be what they seem.

IAGO

Why, then, I think Cassio's an honest man.

OTHELLO

Nay, yet there's more in this:
I prithee, speak to me as to thy thinkings,
As thou dost ruminate, and give thy worst of thoughts
The worst of words.

IAGO

Good my lord, pardon me:
Though I am bound to every act of duty,
I am not bound to that all slaves are free to.
Utter my thoughts? Why, say they are vile and false; As where's
that palace whereinto foul things Sometimes intrude not? who has
a breast so pure, But some uncleanly apprehensions
Keep leets and law–days and in session sit
With meditations lawful?

OTHELLO

Thou dost conspire against thy friend, Iago,
If thou but think'st him wrong'd and makest his ear
A stranger to thy thoughts.

IAGO

I do beseech you—
Though I perchance am vicious in my guess, As, I
confess, it is my nature's plague
To spy into abuses, and oft my jealousy
Shapes faults that are not—that your wisdom yet, From one
that so imperfectly conceits,
Would take no notice, nor build yourself a trouble
Out of his scattering and unsure observance. It were not
for your quiet nor your good,
Nor for my manhood, honesty, or wisdom, To let you
know my thoughts.

OTHELLO

What dost thou mean?

IAGO

Good name in man and woman, dear my lord,

Is the immediate jewel of their souls:
Who steals my purse steals trash; 'tis something, nothing;
'Twas mine, 'tis his, and has been slave to thousands: But he that
filches from me my good name
Robs me of that which not enriches him
And makes me poor indeed.

OTHELLO

By heaven, I'll know thy thoughts.

IAGO

You cannot, if my heart were in your hand; Nor shall
not, whilst 'tis in my custody.

OTHELLO

Ha!

IAGO

O, beware, my lord, of jealousy;
It is the green–eyed monster which doth mock The meat it
feeds on; that cuckold lives in bliss Who, certain of his fate,
loves not his wronger; But, O, what damned minutes tells he
o'er
Who dotes, yet doubts, suspects, yet strongly loves!

OTHELLO

O misery!

IAGO

Poor and content is rich and rich enough, But riches
fineless is as poor as winter
To him that ever fears he shall be poor.
Good heaven, the souls of all my tribe defend

From jealousy!

OTHELLO

Why, why is this?
Think'st thou I'ld make a lie of jealousy, To follow
still the changes of the moon
With fresh suspicions? No; to be once in doubt Is once to be
resolved: exchange me for a goat, When I shall turn the
business of my soul
To such exsufflicate and blown surmises,
Matching thy inference. 'Tis not to make me jealous
To say my wife is fair, feeds well, loves company, Is free of
speech, sings, plays and dances well; Where virtue is, these are
more virtuous:
Nor from mine own weak merits will I draw
The smallest fear or doubt of her revolt; For she had
eyes, and chose me. No, Iago; I'll see before I doubt;
when I doubt, prove;
And on the proof, there is no more but this,— Away at
once with love or jealousy!

IAGO

I am glad of it; for now I shall have reason To show the
love and duty that I bear you With franker spirit: therefore,
as I am bound, Receive it from me. I speak not yet of
proof.
Look to your wife; observe her well with Cassio; Wear your
eye thus, not jealous nor secure:
I would not have your free and noble nature, Out of self–
bounty, be abused; look to't:
I know our country disposition well;
In Venice they do let heaven see the pranks

They dare not show their husbands; their best conscience
Is not to leave't undone, but keep't unknown.

OTHELLO

Dost thou say so?

IAGO

She did deceive her father, marrying you;
And when she seem'd to shake and fear your looks, She loved
them most.

OTHELLO

And so she did.

IAGO

Why, go to then;
She that, so young, could give out such a seeming, To seal her
father's eyes up close as oak–
He thought 'twas witchcraft—but I am much to blame; I humbly do
beseech you of your pardon
For too much loving you.

OTHELLO

I am bound to thee for ever.

IAGO

I see this hath a little dash'd your spirits.

OTHELLO

Not a jot, not a jot.

IAGO

I' faith, I fear it has.
I hope you will consider what is spoke
Comes from my love. But I do see you're moved:

I am to pray you not to strain my speech To grosser
issues nor to larger reach Than to suspicion.

OTHELLO

    I will not.

IAGO

Should you do so, my lord,
My speech should fall into such vile success
As my thoughts aim not at. Cassio's my worthy friend— My lord, I
see you're moved.

OTHELLO

No, not much moved:
I do not think but Desdemona's honest.

IAGO

Long live she so! and long live you to think so!

OTHELLO

And yet, how nature erring from itself,—

IAGO

Ay, there's the point: as—to be bold with you— Not to affect
many proposed matches
Of her own clime, complexion, and degree, Whereto we
see in all things nature tends— Foh! one may smell in such
a will most rank, Foul disproportion thoughts unnatural.
But pardon me; I do not in position
Distinctly speak of her; though I may fear

Her will, recoiling to her better judgment, May fall to
match you with her country forms And happily repent.

OTHELLO

Farewell, farewell:
If more thou dost perceive, let me know more; Set on thy
wife to observe: leave me, Iago:

IAGO

[Going] My lord, I take my leave.

OTHELLO

Why did I marry? This honest creature doubtless
Sees and knows more, much more, than he unfolds.

IAGO

[Returning] My lord, I would I might entreat your honour To scan this thing
no further; leave it to time: Though it be fit that Cassio have his place, For
sure, he fills it up with great ability, Yet, if you please to hold him off
awhile, You shall by that perceive him and his means: Note, if your lady
strain his entertainment With any strong or vehement importunity; Much
will be seen in that. In the mean time, Let me be thought too busy in my
fears— As worthy cause I have to fear I am— And hold her free, I do
beseech your honour.

OTHELLO

Fear not my government.

IAGO

I once more take my leave. [*Exit*]

OTHELLO

This fellow's of exceeding honesty,
And knows all qualities, with a learned spirit, Of human
dealings. If I do prove her haggard, Though that her jesses
were my dear heartstrings, I'ld whistle her off and let her down
the wind,
To pray at fortune. Haply, for I am black
And have not those soft parts of conversation That
chamberers have, or for I am declined Into the vale of
years,—yet that's not much— She's gone. I am abused; and
my relief
Must be to loathe her. O curse of marriage, That we can call
these delicate creatures ours, And not their appetites! I had
rather be a toad, And live upon the vapour of a dungeon,
Than keep a corner in the thing I love
For others' uses. Yet, 'tis the plague of great ones; Prerogatived
are they less than the base;
'Tis destiny unshunnable, like death:
Even then this forked plague is fated to us
When we do quicken. Desdemona comes:

Re–enter DESDEMONA and EMILIA

If she be false, O, then heaven mocks itself! I'll not
believe't.

DESDEMONA

How now, my dear Othello!
Your dinner, and the generous islanders
By you invited, do attend your presence.

OTHELLO

I am to blame.

DESDEMONA

Why do you speak so faintly? Are you not
well?

OTHELLO

I have a pain upon my forehead here.

DESDEMONA

'Faith, that's with watching; 'twill away again: Let me but
bind it hard, within this hour
It will be well.

OTHELLO

Your napkin is too little:

He puts the handkerchief from him; and it drops

Let it alone. Come, I'll go in with you.

DESDEMONA

I am very sorry that you are not well. [*Exeunt

OTHELLO and DESDEMONA] **EMILIA**

I am glad I have found this napkin:
This was her first remembrance from the Moor: My wayward
husband hath a hundred times Woo'd me to steal it; but she so
loves the token, For he conjured her she should ever keep it,
That she reserves it evermore about her

To kiss and talk to. I'll have the work ta'en out,

And give't Iago: what he will do with it
Heaven knows, not I;
I nothing but to please his fantasy.

Re–enter Iago

IAGO

How now! what do you here alone?

EMILIA

Do not you chide; I have a thing for you.

IAGO

A thing for me? it is a common thing—

EMILIA

       Ha!

IAGO

To have a foolish wife.

EMILIA

O, is that all? What will you give me now
For the same handkerchief?

IAGO

What handkerchief?

EMILIA

What handkerchief?
Why, that the Moor first gave to Desdemona; That which
so often you did bid me steal.

IAGO

Hast stol'n it from her?

EMILIA

No, 'faith; she let it drop by negligence.
And, to the advantage, I, being here, took't up. Look, here it
is.

IAGO

A good wench; give it me.

EMILIA

What will you do with 't, that you have been so earnest To have me filch it?

IAGO

[Snatching it] Why, what's that to you?

EMILIA

If it be not for some purpose of import, Give't me
again: poor lady, she'll run mad When she shall lack it.

IAGO

Be not acknown on 't; I have use for it. Go, leave
me.

[*Exit EMILIA*]

I will in Cassio's lodging lose this napkin, And let him
find it. Trifles light as air
Are to the jealous confirmations strong

As proofs of holy writ: this may do something. The Moor
already changes with my poison: Dangerous conceits are, in
their natures, poisons. Which at the first are scarce found to
distaste,
But with a little act upon the blood.
Burn like the mines of Sulphur. I did say so: Look, where
he comes!

Re–enter OTHELLO

Not poppy, nor mandragora,
Nor all the drowsy syrups of the world, Shall ever
medicine thee to that sweet sleep Which thou owedst
yesterday.

OTHELLO

Ha! ha! false to me?

IAGO

Why, how now, general! no more of that.

OTHELLO

Avaunt! be gone! thou hast set me on the rack: I swear 'tis
better to be much abused
Than but to know't a little.

IAGO

How now, my lord!

OTHELLO

What sense had I of her stol'n hours of lust? I saw't not,
thought it not, it harm'd not me:
I slept the next night well, was free and merry; I found not
Cassio's kisses on her lips:

He that is robb'd, not wanting what is stol'n, Let him not know't, and he's not robb'd at all.

IAGO

I am sorry to hear this.

OTHELLO

I had been happy, if the general camp, Pioners and all, had tasted her sweet body, So I had nothing known. O, now, for ever
Farewell the tranquil mind! farewell content! Farewell the plumed troop, and the big wars, That make ambition virtue! O, farewell!
Farewell the neighing steed, and the shrill trump, The spirit–stirring drum, the ear–piercing fife, The royal banner, and all quality,
Pride, pomp and circumstance of glorious war! And, O you mortal engines, whose rude throats The immortal Jove's dead clamours counterfeit, Farewell! Othello's occupation's gone!

IAGO

Is't possible, my lord?

OTHELLO

Villain, be sure thou prove my love a whore, Be sure of it; give me the ocular proof:
Or by the worth of man's eternal soul,
Thou hadst been better have been born a dog
Than answer my waked wrath!

IAGO

Is't come to this?

OTHELLO

Make me to see't; or, at the least, so prove it, That the
probation bear no hinge nor loop
To hang a doubt on; or woe upon thy life!

IAGO

My noble lord,—

OTHELLO

If thou dost slander her and torture me, Never pray
more; abandon all remorse; On horror's head horrors
accumulate;
Do deeds to make heaven weep, all earth amazed; For nothing
canst thou to damnation add
Greater than that.

IAGO

O grace! O heaven forgive me!
Are you a man? have you a soul or sense?
God be wi' you; take mine office. O wretched fool. That livest to
make thine honesty a vice!
O monstrous world! Take note, take note, O world, To be direct
and honest is not safe.
I thank you for this profit; and from hence
I'll love no friend, sith love breeds such offence.

OTHELLO

Nay, stay: thou shouldst be honest.

IAGO

I should be wise, for honesty's a fool
And loses that it works for.

OTHELLO

By the world,
I think my wife be honest and think she is not; I think that
thou art just and think thou art not.
I'll have some proof. Her name, that was as fresh
As Dian's visage, is now begrimed and black As mine own
face. If there be cords, or knives, Poison, or fire, or
suffocating streams,
I'll not endure it. Would I were satisfied!

IAGO

I see, sir, you are eaten up with passion: I do repent
me that I put it to you.
You would be satisfied?

OTHELLO

Would! nay, I will.

IAGO

And may: but, how? how satisfied, my lord? Would you,
the supervisor, grossly gape on— Behold her topp'd?

OTHELLO

Death and damnation! O!

IAGO

It were a tedious difficulty, I think,
To bring them to that prospect: damn them then, If ever
mortal eyes do see them bolster
More than their own! What then? how then? What shall I
say? Where's satisfaction?

It is impossible you should see this,
Were they as prime as goats, as hot as monkeys, As salt as
wolves in pride, and fools as gross
As ignorance made drunk. But yet, I say, If imputation
and strong circumstances, Which lead directly to the
door of truth, Will give you satisfaction, you may have't.

OTHELLO

Give me a living reason she's disloyal.

IAGO

I do not like the office:
But, sith I am enter'd in this cause so far, Prick'd to't
by foolish honesty and love,
I will go on. I lay with Cassio lately; And, being
troubled with a raging tooth, I could not sleep.
There are a kind of men so loose of soul, That in their
sleeps will mutter their affairs: One of this kind is Cassio:
In sleep I heard him say 'Sweet Desdemona, Let us be
wary, let us hide our loves;'
And then, sir, would he gripe and wring my hand, Cry 'O sweet
creature!' and then kiss me hard,
As if he pluck'd up kisses by the roots
That grew upon my lips: then laid his leg
Over my thigh, and sigh'd, and kiss'd; and then
Cried 'Cursed fate that gave thee to the Moor!'

OTHELLO

O monstrous! monstrous!

IAGO

Nay, this was but his dream.

OTHELLO

But this denoted a foregone conclusion:
'Tis a shrewd doubt, though it be but a dream.

IAGO

And this may help to thicken other proofs
That do demonstrate thinly.

OTHELLO

I'll tear her all to pieces.

IAGO

Nay, but be wise: yet we see nothing done; She may be
honest yet. Tell me but this,
Have you not sometimes seen a handkerchief
Spotted with strawberries in your wife's hand?

OTHELLO

I gave her such a one; 'twas my first gift.

IAGO

I know not that; but such a handkerchief— I am sure it
was your wife's—did I to–day See Cassio wipe his beard
with.

OTHELLO

If it be that—

IAGO

If it be that, or any that was hers,
It speaks against her with the other proofs.

OTHELLO

O, that the slave had forty thousand lives! One is too
poor, too weak for my revenge. Now do I see 'tis true.
Look here, Iago;
All my fond love thus do I blow to heaven.
'Tis gone.
Arise, black vengeance, from thy hollow cell! Yield up, O
love, thy crown and hearted throne
To tyrannous hate! Swell, bosom, with thy fraught, For 'tis of
aspics' tongues!

IAGO

Yet be content.

OTHELLO

O, blood, blood, blood!

IAGO

Patience, I say; your mind perhaps may change.

OTHELLO

Never, Iago: Like to the Pontic sea, Whose icy current
and compulsive course Ne'er feels retiring ebb, but
keeps due on To the Propontic and the Hellespont,
Even so my bloody thoughts, with violent pace, Shall ne'er
look back, ne'er ebb to humble love, Till that a capable and
wide revenge
Swallow them up. Now, by yond marble heaven,

Kneels

In the due reverence of a sacred vow
I here engage my words.

IAGO

Do not rise yet.

Kneels

Witness, you ever–burning lights above, You
elements that clip us round about, Witness that here
Iago doth give up
The execution of his wit, hands, heart,
To wrong'd Othello's service! Let him command, And to obey
shall be in me remorse,
What bloody business ever.

They rise

OTHELLO

I greet thy love,
Not with vain thanks, but with acceptance bounteous, And will
upon the instant put thee to't:
Within these three days let me hear thee say
That Cassio's not alive.

IAGO

My friend is dead; 'tis done at your request: But let her
live.

OTHELLO

Damn her, lewd minx! O, damn her! Come, go with
me apart; I will withdraw,

To furnish me with some swift means of death
For the fair devil. Now art thou my lieutenant.

IAGO

I am your own for ever. [*Exeunt*]

Scene IV

Before the Castle

[*Enter DESDEMONA, EMILIA, and Clown*]

DESDEMONA

Do you know, sirrah, where Lieutenant Cassio lies?

Clown

I dare not say he lies any where.

DESDEMONA

Why, man?

Clown

He's a soldier, and for one to say a soldier lies, is stabbing.

DESDEMONA

Go to: where lodges he?

Clown

To tell you where he lodges, is to tell you where I lie.

DESDEMONA

Can any thing be made of this?

Clown

I know not where he lodges, and for me to devise a lodging and say he lies here or he lies there, were to lie in mine own throat.

DESDEMONA

Can you inquire him out, and be edified by report?

Clown

I will catechise the world for him; that is, make questions, and by them answer.

DESDEMONA

Seek him, bid him come hither: tell him I have moved my lord on his behalf, and hope all will be well.

Clown

To do this is within the compass of man's wit: and therefore I will attempt the doing it. [*Exit*]

DESDEMONA

Where should I lose that handkerchief, Emilia?

EMILIA

I know not, madam.

DESDEMONA

> Believe me, I had rather have lost my purse
> Full of crusadoes: and, but my noble Moor
> Is true of mind and made of no such baseness
> As jealous creatures are, it were enough
> To put him to ill thinking.

EMILIA

Is he not jealous?

DESDEMONA

Who, he? I think the sun where he was born
Drew all such humours from him.

EMILIA

Look, where he comes.

DESDEMONA

I will not leave him now till Cassio
Be call'd to him. [*Enter*

OTHELLO]

How is't with you, my lord

OTHELLO

Well, my good lady.

Aside

O, hardness to dissemble!— How do you,
Desdemona?

DESDEMONA

Well, my good lord.

OTHELLO

Give me your hand: this hand is moist, my lady.

DESDEMONA

It yet hath felt no age nor known no sorrow.

OTHELLO

This argues fruitfulness and liberal heart:
Hot, hot, and moist: this hand of yours requires A sequester
from liberty, fasting and prayer, Much castigation, exercise
devout;
For here's a young and sweating devil here, That
commonly rebels. 'Tis a good hand,
A frank one.

DESDEMONA

You may, indeed, say so;
For 'twas that hand that gave away my heart.

OTHELLO

A liberal hand: the hearts of old gave hands; But our new
heraldry is hands, not hearts.

DESDEMONA

I cannot speak of this. Come now, your promise.

OTHELLO

What promise, chuck?

DESDEMONA

I have sent to bid Cassio come speak with you.

OTHELLO

I have a salt and sorry rheum offends me; Lend me thy
handkerchief.

DESDEMONA

Here, my lord.

OTHELLO

That which I gave you.

DESDEMONA

I have it not about me.

OTHELLO

Not?

DESDEMONA

No, indeed, my lord.

OTHELLO

That is a fault. That handkerchief Did an Egyptian to my mother give; She was a charmer, and could almost read The thoughts of people: she told her, while she kept it, 'Twould make her amiable and subdue my father Entirely to her love, but if she lost it Or made gift of it, my father's eye Should hold her loathed and his spirits should hunt After new fancies: she, dying, gave it me; And bid me, when my fate would have me wive, To give it her. I did so: and take heed on't; Make it a darling like your precious eye; To lose't or give't away were such perdition As nothing else could match.

DESDEMONA

Is't possible?

OTHELLO

'Tis true: there's magic in the web of it: A sibyl, that
had number'd in the world
The sun to course two hundred compasses, In her
prophetic fury sew'd the work;
The worms were hallow'd that did breed the silk;

And it was dyed in mummy which the skilful
Conserved of maidens' hearts.

DESDEMONA

Indeed! is't true?

OTHELLO

Most veritable; therefore look to't well.

DESDEMONA

Then would to God that I had never seen't!

OTHELLO

Ha! wherefore?

DESDEMONA

Why do you speak so startingly and rash?

OTHELLO

Is't lost? is't gone? speak, is it out o' the way?

DESDEMONA

Heaven bless us!

OTHELLO

Say you?

DESDEMONA

It is not lost; but what an if it were?

OTHELLO

How!

DESDEMONA

I say, it is not lost.

OTHELLO

Fetch't, let me see't.

DESDEMONA

Why, so I can, sir, but I will not now. This is a trick
to put me from my suit: Pray you, let Cassio be
received again.

OTHELLO

Fetch me the handkerchief: my mind misgives.

DESDEMONA

Come, come;
You'll never meet a more sufficient man.

OTHELLO

The handkerchief!

DESDEMONA

I pray, talk me of Cassio.

OTHELLO

The handkerchief!

DESDEMONA

A man that all his time

Hath founded his good fortunes on your love, Shared
dangers with you,—

OTHELLO

The handkerchief!

DESDEMONA

In sooth, you are to blame.

OTHELLO

Away! [*Exit*]

EMILIA

Is not this man jealous?

DESDEMONA

I ne'er saw this before.
Sure, there's some wonder in this handkerchief: I am most
unhappy in the loss of it.

EMILIA

'Tis not a year or two shows us a man:
They are all but stomachs, and we all but food; To eat us
hungerly, and when they are full,
They belch us. Look you, Cassio and my husband! [*Enter

CASSIO and IAGO*]

IAGO

There is no other way; 'tis she must do't:
And, lo, the happiness! go, and importune her.

DESDEMONA

How now, good Cassio! what's the news with you?

CASSIO

Madam, my former suit: I do beseech you That by your
virtuous means I may again Exist, and be a member of
his love
Whom I with all the office of my heart Entirely
honour: I would not be delay'd. If my offence be of
such mortal kind
That nor my service past, nor present sorrows, Nor
purposed merit in futurity,
Can ransom me into his love again, But to know
so must be my benefit;
So shall I clothe me in a forced content, And shut
myself up in some other course, To fortune's alms.

DESDEMONA

Alas, thrice–gentle Cassio!
My advocation is not now in tune;
My lord is not my lord; nor should I know him, Were he in
favour as in humour alter'd.
So help me every spirit sanctified,
As I have spoken for you all my best
And stood within the blank of his displeasure For my free
speech! you must awhile be patient: What I can do I will; and
more I will
Than for myself I dare: let that suffice you.

IAGO

Is my lord angry?

EMILIA

He went hence but now,
And certainly in strange unquietness.

IAGO

Can he be angry? I have seen the cannon, When it hath
blown his ranks into the air, And, like the devil, from his
very arm
Puff'd his own brother:—and can he be angry? Something of
moment then: I will go meet him: There's matter in't indeed,
if he be angry.

DESDEMONA

I prithee, do so. [*Exit IAGO*]

Something, sure, of state,
Either from Venice, or some unhatch'd practise Made
demonstrable here in Cyprus to him, Hath puddled his clear
spirit: and in such cases Men's natures wrangle with inferior
things,
Though great ones are their object. 'Tis even so; For let our
finger ache, and it indues
Our other healthful members even to that sense Of pain: nay,
we must think men are not gods, Nor of them look for such
observances
As fit the bridal. Beshrew me much, Emilia, I was,
unhandsome warrior as I am, Arraigning his unkindness
with my soul;
But now I find I had suborn'd the witness, And he's

indicted falsely.

EMILIA

Pray heaven it be state–matters, as you think,

And no conception nor no jealous toy
Concerning you.

DESDEMONA

Alas the day! I never gave him cause.

EMILIA

But jealous souls will not be answer'd so; They are not
ever jealous for the cause,
But jealous for they are jealous: 'tis a monster
Begot upon itself, born on itself.

DESDEMONA

Heaven keep that monster from Othello's mind!

EMILIA

Lady, amen.

DESDEMONA

I will go seek him. Cassio, walk hereabout: If I do find
him fit, I'll move your suit
And seek to effect it to my uttermost.

CASSIO

I humbly thank your ladyship. [*Exeunt*

DESDEMONA and EMILIA] [*Enter BIANCA*]

BIANCA

Save you, friend Cassio!

CASSIO

What make you from home?
How is it with you, my most fair Bianca?
I' faith, sweet love, I was coming to your house.

BIANCA

And I was going to your lodging, Cassio.
What, keep a week away? seven days and nights? Eight score
eight hours? and lovers' absent hours, More tedious than the dial
eight score times?
O weary reckoning!

CASSIO

Pardon me, Bianca:
I have this while with leaden thoughts been press'd: But I shall,
in a more continuate time,
Strike off this score of absence. Sweet Bianca,

Giving her DESDEMONA's handkerchief

Take me this work out.

BIANCA

O Cassio, whence came this?
This is some token from a newer friend: To the felt
absence now I feel a cause: Is't come to this? Well,
well.

CASSIO

Go to, woman!
Throw your vile guesses in the devil's teeth,
From whence you have them. You are jealous now
That this is from some mistress, some remembrance:

No, in good troth, Bianca.

BIANCA

Why, whose is it?

CASSIO

I know not, sweet: I found it in my chamber. I like the
work well: ere it be demanded— As like enough it will—
I'ld have it copied: Take it, and do't; and leave me for this
time.

BIANCA

Leave you! wherefore?

CASSIO

I do attend here on the general;
And think it no addition, nor my wish, To have him
see me woman'd.

BIANCA

Why, I pray you?

CASSIO

Not that I love you not.

BIANCA

But that you do not love me.
I pray you, bring me on the way a little, And say if I
shall see you soon at night.

CASSIO

'Tis but a little way that I can bring you;

For I attend here: but I'll see you soon.

BIANCA

'Tis very good; I must be circumstanced. [*Exeunt*]

ACT IV

Scene I

Cyprus. Before the Castle

[*Enter OTHELLO and IAGO*]

IAGO

Will you think so?

OTHELLO

Think so, Iago!

IAGO

What,
To kiss in private?

OTHELLO

An unauthorized kiss.

IAGO

Or to be naked with her friend in bed
An hour or more, not meaning any harm?

OTHELLO

Naked in bed, Iago, and not mean harm! It is
hypocrisy against the devil:
They that mean virtuously, and yet do so,
The devil their virtue tempts, and they tempt heaven.

IAGO

So they do nothing, 'tis a venial slip: But if I give my
wife a handkerchief,—

OTHELLO

What then?

IAGO

Why, then, 'tis hers, my lord; and, being hers, She may, I
think, bestow't on any man.

OTHELLO

She is protectress of her honour too: May she give
that?

IAGO

Her honour is an essence that's not seen; They have it
very oft that have it not: But, for the handkerchief,—

OTHELLO

By heaven, I would most gladly have forgot it. Thou said'st,
it comes o'er my memory,
As doth the raven o'er the infected house, Boding to
all—he had my handkerchief.

IAGO

Ay, what of that?

OTHELLO

That's not so good now.

IAGO

What,
If I had said I had seen him do you wrong?
Or heard him say,—as knaves be such abroad, Who having,
by their own importunate suit,
Or voluntary dotage of some mistress, Convinced or
supplied them, cannot choose But they must blab—

OTHELLO

Hath he said any thing?

IAGO

He hath, my lord; but be you well assured, No more
than he'll unswear.

OTHELLO

What hath he said?

IAGO

'Faith, that he did—I know not what he did.

OTHELLO

What? what?

IAGO

Lie—

OTHELLO

With her?

IAGO

With her, on her; what you will.

OTHELLO

Lie with her! lie on her! We say lie on her, when they belie her. Lie with her!
that's fulsome. —Handkerchief—confessions— handkerchief!—To confess,
and be hanged for his labour;— first, to be hanged, and then to confess.—I
tremble at it. Nature would not invest herself in such shadowing passion
without some instruction. It is not words that shake me thus. Pish! Noses,
ears, and lips. —Is't possible?—Confess—handkerchief!
—O devil!— *Falls in a*

trance **IAGO**

Work on,
My medicine, work! Thus credulous fools are caught; And many
worthy and chaste dames even thus,
All guiltless, meet reproach. What, ho! my lord! My lord, I
say! Othello!

[*Enter CASSIO*]

How now, Cassio!

CASSIO

What's the matter?

IAGO

My lord is fall'n into an epilepsy:
This is his second fit; he had one yesterday.

CASSIO

Rub him about the temples.

IAGO

No, forbear;
The lethargy must have his quiet course: If not, he foams
at mouth and by and by Breaks out to savage madness.
Look he stirs: Do you withdraw yourself a little while,
He will recover straight: when he is gone,
I would on great occasion speak with you. [*Exit*

CASSIO]

How is it, general? have you not hurt your head?

OTHELLO

Dost thou mock me?

IAGO

I mock you! no, by heaven.
Would you would bear your fortune like a man!

OTHELLO

A horned man's a monster and a beast.

IAGO

There's many a beast then in a populous city, And many a
civil monster.

OTHELLO

Did he confess it?

IAGO

Good sir, be a man;
Think every bearded fellow that's but yoked
May draw with you: there's millions now alive

That nightly lie in those unproper beds
Which they dare swear peculiar: your case is better. O, 'tis the
spite of hell, the fiend's arch–mock,
To lip a wanton in a secure couch,
And to suppose her chaste! No, let me know;
And knowing what I am, I know what she shall be.

OTHELLO

O, thou art wise; 'tis certain.

IAGO

Stand you awhile apart;
Confine yourself but in a patient list.
Whilst you were here o'erwhelmed with your grief— A passion
most unsuiting such a man—
Cassio came hither: I shifted him away, And laid
good 'scuse upon your ecstasy,
Bade him anon return and here speak with me; The which he
promised. Do but encave yourself, And mark the fleers, the
gibes, and notable scorns, That dwell in every region of his face;
For I will make him tell the tale anew,
Where, how, how oft, how long ago, and when
He hath, and is again to cope your wife:
I say, but mark his gesture. Marry, patience; Or I shall say
you are all in all in spleen, And nothing of a man.

OTHELLO

Dost thou hear, Iago?
I will be found most cunning in my patience; But—dost
thou hear?—most bloody.

IAGO

That's not amiss;
But yet keep time in all. Will you withdraw?

OTHELLO retires

Now will I question Cassio of Bianca, A housewife
that by selling her desires
Buys herself bread and clothes: it is a creature That dotes on
Cassio; as 'tis the strumpet's plague To beguile many and be
beguiled by one:
He, when he hears of her, cannot refrain
From the excess of laughter. Here he comes:

Re–enter CASSIO

As he shall smile, Othello shall go mad; And his
unbookish jealousy must construe
Poor Cassio's smiles, gestures and light behavior, Quite in the
wrong. How do you now, lieutenant?

CASSIO

The worser that you give me the addition
Whose want even kills me.

IAGO

Ply Desdemona well, and you are sure on't.

Speaking lower

Now, if this suit lay in Bianco's power, How quickly
should you speed!

CASSIO

Alas, poor caitiff!

OTHELLO

Look, how he laughs already!

IAGO

I never knew woman love man so.

CASSIO

Alas, poor rogue! I think, i' faith, she loves me.

OTHELLO

Now he denies it faintly, and laughs it out.

IAGO

Do you hear, Cassio?

OTHELLO

Now he importunes him
To tell it o'er: go to; well said, well said.

IAGO

She gives it out that you shall marry hey: Do you
intend it?

CASSIO

Ha, ha, ha!

OTHELLO

Do you triumph, Roman? do you triumph?

CASSIO

I marry her! what? a customer! Prithee, bear some charity to my wit: do not
think it so unwholesome. Ha, ha, ha!

OTHELLO

So, so, so, so: they laugh that win.

IAGO

'Faith, the cry goes that you shall marry her.

CASSIO

Prithee, say true.

IAGO

I am a very villain else.

OTHELLO

Have you scored me? Well.

CASSIO

This is the monkey's own giving out: she is persuaded I will marry her, out of her own love and flattery, not out of my promise.

OTHELLO

Iago beckons me; now he begins the story.

CASSIO

She was here even now; she haunts me in every place. I was the other day talking on the sea–bank with certain Venetians; and thither comes the bauble, and, by this hand, she falls me thus about my neck—

OTHELLO

Crying 'O dear Cassio!' as it were: his gesture imports it.

CASSIO

So hangs, and lolls, and weeps upon me; so hales, and pulls me:
ha, ha, ha!

OTHELLO

Now he tells how she plucked him to my chamber. O, I see that nose of
yours, but not that dog I shall throw it to.

CASSIO

Well, I must leave her company.

IAGO

Before me! look, where she comes.

CASSIO

'Tis such another fitchew! marry a perfumed one. [*Enter*

BIANCA]

What do you mean by this haunting of me?

BIANCA

Let the devil and his dam haunt you! What did you mean by that same
handkerchief you gave me even now? I was a fine fool to take it. I must take
out the work?—A likely piece of work, that you should find it in your
chamber, and not know who left it there! This is some minx's token, and I
must take out the work? There; give it your hobby–horse: wheresoever you
had it, I'll take out no work on't.

CASSIO

How now, my sweet Bianca! how now! how now!

OTHELLO

By heaven, that should be my handkerchief!

BIANCA

An you'll come to supper to–night, you may; an you will not, come when you are next prepared for.

[*Exit*]

IAGO

After her, after her.

CASSIO

'Faith, I must; she'll rail in the street else.

IAGO

Will you sup there?

CASSIO

'Faith, I intend so.

IAGO

Well, I may chance to see you; for I would very fain speak with you.

CASSIO

Prithee, come; will you?

IAGO

Go to; say no more. [*Exit*

CASSIO] **OTHELLO**

[Advancing] How shall I murder him, Iago?

IAGO

Did you perceive how he laughed at his vice?

OTHELLO

O Iago!

IAGO

And did you see the handkerchief?

OTHELLO

Was that mine?

IAGO

Yours by this hand: and to see how he prizes the foolish woman your wife! she gave it him, and he hath given it his whore.

OTHELLO

I would have him nine years a–killing.
A fine woman! a fair woman! a sweet woman!

IAGO

Nay, you must forget that.

OTHELLO

Ay, let her rot, and perish, and be damned to–night; for she shall not live: no, my heart is turned to stone; I strike it, and it hurts my hand. O, the world hath not a sweeter creature: she might lie by an emperor's side and command him tasks.

IAGO

Nay, that's not your way.

OTHELLO

Hang her! I do but say what she is: so delicate with her needle: an admirable musician: O! she will sing the savageness out of a bear: of so high and plenteous wit and invention:—

IAGO

She's the worse for all this.

OTHELLO

O, a thousand thousand times: and then, of so gentle a condition!

IAGO

Ay, too gentle.

OTHELLO

Nay, that's certain: but yet the pity of it, Iago! O Iago, the pity of it, Iago!

IAGO

If you are so fond over her iniquity, give her patent to offend; for, if it touch not you, it comes near nobody.

OTHELLO

I will chop her into messes: cuckold me!

IAGO

O, 'tis foul in her.

OTHELLO

With mine officer!

IAGO

That's fouler.

OTHELLO

Get me some poison, Iago; this night: I'll not expostulate with her, lest her body and beauty unprovide my mind again: this night, Iago.

IAGO

Do it not with poison, strangle her in her bed, even the bed she hath contaminated.

OTHELLO

Good, good: the justice of it pleases: very good.

IAGO

And for Cassio, let me be his undertaker: you shall hear more by midnight.

OTHELLO

Excellent good.

A trumpet within

What trumpet is that same?

IAGO

> Something from Venice, sure. 'Tis Lodovico
> Come from the duke: and, see, your wife is with him. [*Enter*

LODOVICO, DESDEMONA, and Attendants]

LODOVICO

Save you, worthy general!

OTHELLO

With all my heart, sir.

LODOVICO

The duke and senators of Venice greet you.

Gives him a letter

OTHELLO

I kiss the instrument of their pleasures. *Opens the letter, and reads* **DESDEMONA**

And what's the news, good cousin Lodovico?

IAGO

I am very glad to see you, signior
Welcome to Cyprus.

LODOVICO

I thank you. How does Lieutenant Cassio?

IAGO

Lives, sir.

DESDEMONA

Cousin, there's fall'n between him and my lord
An unkind breach: but you shall make all well.

OTHELLO

Are you sure of that?

DESDEMONA

My lord?

OTHELLO

[Reads] 'This fail you not to do, as you will—'

LODOVICO

He did not call; he's busy in the paper.
Is there division 'twixt my lord and Cassio?

DESDEMONA

A most unhappy one: I would do much
To atone them, for the love I bear to Cassio.

OTHELLO

Fire and brimstone!

DESDEMONA

My lord?

OTHELLO

Are you wise?

DESDEMONA

What, is he angry?

LODOVICO

May be the letter moved him;
For, as I think, they do command him home, Deputing
Cassio in his government.

DESDEMONA

Trust me, I am glad on't.

OTHELLO

Indeed!

DESDEMONA

My lord?

OTHELLO

I am glad to see you mad.

DESDEMONA

Why, sweet Othello,—

OTHELLO

[Striking her] Devil!

DESDEMONA

I have not deserved this.

LODOVICO

My lord, this would not be believed in Venice, Though I
should swear I saw't: 'tis very much: Make her amends; she
weeps.

OTHELLO

O devil, devil!
If that the earth could teem with woman's tears, Each drop
she falls would prove a crocodile. Out of my sight!

DESDEMONA

I will not stay to offend you.

Going

LODOVICO

Truly, an obedient lady:
I do beseech your lordship, call her back.

OTHELLO

Mistress!

DESDEMONA

My lord?

OTHELLO

What would you with her, sir?

LODOVICO

Who, I, my lord?

OTHELLO

Ay; you did wish that I would make her turn: Sir, she can
turn, and turn, and yet go on,
And turn again; and she can weep, sir, weep; And she's
obedient, as you say, obedient, Very obedient. Proceed
you in your tears.

Concerning this, sir,—O well–painted passion!— I am
commanded home. Get you away;
I'll send for you anon. Sir, I obey the mandate, And will
return to Venice. Hence, avaunt!

[*Exit DESDEMONA*]

Cassio shall have my place. And, sir, tonight, I do entreat
that we may sup together:
You are welcome, sir, to Cyprus.—Goats and monkeys! [*Exit*]

LODOVICO

Is this the noble Moor whom our full senate
Call all in all sufficient? Is this the nature
Whom passion could not shake? whose solid virtue
The shot of accident, nor dart of chance, Could
neither graze nor pierce?

IAGO

He is much changed.

LODOVICO

Are his wits safe? is he not light of brain?

IAGO

He's that he is: I may not breathe my censure What he might
be: if what he might he is not, I would to heaven he were!

LODOVICO

What, strike his wife!

IAGO

'Faith, that was not so well; yet would I knew
That stroke would prove the worst!

LODOVICO

Is it his use?
Or did the letters work upon his blood, And new–
create this fault?

IAGO

Alas, alas!
It is not honesty in me to speak
What I have seen and known. You shall observe him, And his own
courses will denote him so
That I may save my speech: do but go after, And mark
how he continues.

LODOVICO

I am sorry that I am deceived in him. [*Exeunt*]

SCENE II

A Room in the Castle

[*Enter OTHELLO and EMILIA*]

OTHELLO

You have seen nothing then?

EMILIA

Nor ever heard, nor ever did suspect.

OTHELLO

Yes, you have seen Cassio and she together.

EMILIA

But then I saw no harm, and then I heard
Each syllable that breath made up between them.

OTHELLO

What, did they never whisper?

EMILIA

Never, my lord.

OTHELLO

Nor send you out o' the way?

EMILIA

Never.

OTHELLO

To fetch her fan, her gloves, her mask, nor nothing?

EMILIA

Never, my lord.

OTHELLO

That's strange.

EMILIA

I durst, my lord, to wager she is honest,
Lay down my soul at stake: if you think other, Remove your
thought; it doth abuse your bosom. If any wretch have put this
in your head,
Let heaven requite it with the serpent's curse! For, if she be
not honest, chaste, and true, There's no man happy; the purest
of their wives Is foul as slander.

OTHELLO

Bid her come hither: go. [*Exit

EMILIA]

She says enough; yet she's a simple bawd
That cannot say as much. This is a subtle whore, A closet lock
and key of villanous secrets
And yet she'll kneel and pray; I have seen her do't. [*Enter

DESDEMONA with EMILIA]

DESDEMONA

My lord, what is your will?

OTHELLO

Pray, chuck, come hither.

DESDEMONA

What is your pleasure?

OTHELLO

Let me see your eyes; Look in my
face.

DESDEMONA

What horrible fancy's this?

OTHELLO

[To EMILIA] Some of your function, mistress; Leave
procreants alone and shut the door; Cough, or cry 'hem,' if
any body come:
Your mystery, your mystery: nay, dispatch. [*Exit*

EMILIA]

DESDEMONA

Upon my knees, what doth your speech import? I understand
a fury in your words.
But not the words.

OTHELLO

Why, what art thou?

DESDEMONA

Your wife, my lord; your true
And loyal wife.

OTHELLO

Come, swear it, damn thyself
Lest, being like one of heaven, the devils themselves Should fear to
seize thee: therefore be double damn'd: Swear thou art honest.

DESDEMONA

Heaven doth truly know it.

OTHELLO

Heaven truly knows that thou art false as hell.

DESDEMONA

To whom, my lord? with whom? how am I false?

OTHELLO

O Desdemona! away! away! away!

DESDEMONA

Alas the heavy day! Why do you weep? Am I the
motive of these tears, my lord? If haply you my father
do suspect
An instrument of this your calling back,
Lay not your blame on me: If you have lost him, Why, I have
lost him too.

OTHELLO

Had it pleased heaven
To try me with affliction; had they rain'd

All kinds of sores and shames on my bare head. Steep'd me in
poverty to the very lips,
Given to captivity me and my utmost hopes,
I should have found in some place of my soul
A drop of patience: but, alas, to make me
A fixed figure for the time of scorn
To point his slow unmoving finger at!
Yet could I bear that too; well, very well:
But there, where I have garner'd up my heart, Where either
I must live, or bear no life;
The fountain from the which my current runs, Or else dries
up; to be discarded thence!
Or keep it as a cistern for foul toads
To knot and gender in! Turn thy complexion there, Patience,
thou young and rose–lipp'd cherubin,— Ay, there, look grim as
hell!

DESDEMONA

I hope my noble lord esteems me honest.

OTHELLO

O, ay; as summer flies are in the shambles, That quicken even with blowing.
O thou weed, Who art so lovely fair and smell'st so sweet That the sense
aches at thee, would thou hadst ne'er been born!

DESDEMONA

Alas, what ignorant sin have I committed?

OTHELLO

Was this fair paper, this most goodly book, Made to write
'whore' upon? What committed! Committed! O thou public
commoner!
I should make very forges of my cheeks,

That would to cinders burn up modesty,
Did I but speak thy deeds. What committed! Heaven stops the
nose at it and the moon winks, The bawdy wind that kisses all
it meets
Is hush'd within the hollow mine of earth, And will not
hear it. What committed! Impudent strumpet!

DESDEMONA

By heaven, you do me wrong.

OTHELLO

Are you not a strumpet?

DESDEMONA

No, as I am a Christian:
If to preserve this vessel for my lord From any
other foul unlawful touch Be not to be a strumpet,
I am none.

OTHELLO

What, not a whore?

DESDEMONA

No, as I shall be saved.

OTHELLO

Is't possible?

DESDEMONA

O, heaven forgive us!

OTHELLO

I cry you mercy, then:
I took you for that cunning whore of Venice
That married with Othello.

Raising his voice

You, mistress,
That have the office opposite to Saint Peter, And keep the
gate of hell!

Re–enter EMILIA

You, you, ay, you!
We have done our course; there's money for your pains: I pray you,
turn the key and keep our counsel.

[*Exit*]

EMILIA

Alas, what does this gentleman conceive?
How do you, madam? how do you, my good lady?

DESDEMONA

'Faith, half asleep.

EMILIA

Good madam, what's the matter with my lord?

DESDEMONA

With who?

EMILIA

Why, with my lord, madam.

DESDEMONA

Who is thy lord?

EMILIA

He that is yours, sweet lady.

DESDEMONA

I have none: do not talk to me, Emilia;
I cannot weep; nor answer have I none,
But what should go by water. Prithee, tonight Lay on my bed
my wedding sheets: remember; And call thy husband hither.

EMILIA

Here's a change indeed! [*Exit*]

DESDEMONA

'Tis meet I should be used so, very meet.
How have I been behaved, that he might stick
The small'st opinion on my least misuse?

Re–enter EMILIA with IAGO

IAGO

What is your pleasure, madam? How is't with
you?

DESDEMONA

I cannot tell. Those that do teach young babes
Do it with gentle means and easy tasks:
He might have chid me so; for, in good faith, I am a child
to chiding.

IAGO

What's the matter, lady?

EMILIA

Alas, Iago, my lord hath so bewhored her. Thrown such
despite and heavy terms upon her, As true hearts cannot bear.

DESDEMONA

Am I that name, Iago?

IAGO

What name, fair lady?

DESDEMONA

Such as she says my lord did say I was.

EMILIA

He call'd her whore: a beggar in his drink
Could not have laid such terms upon his callat.

IAGO

Why did he so?

DESDEMONA

I do not know; I am sure I am none such.

IAGO

Do not weep, do not weep. Alas the day!

EMILIA

Hath she forsook so many noble matches, Her father and
her country and her friends,
To be call'd whore? would it not make one weep?

DESDEMONA

It is my wretched fortune.

IAGO

Beshrew him for't!
How comes this trick upon him?

DESDEMONA

Nay, heaven doth know.

EMILIA

I will be hang'd, if some eternal villain, Some busy
and insinuating rogue,
Some cogging, cozening slave, to get some office, Have not
devised this slander; I'll be hang'd else.

IAGO

Fie, there is no such man; it is impossible.

DESDEMONA

If any such there be, heaven pardon him!

EMILIA

A halter pardon him! and hell gnaw his bones!
Why should he call her whore? who keeps her company? What place?
what time? what form? what likelihood?
The Moor's abused by some most villanous knave, Some base
notorious knave, some scurvy fellow.

O heaven, that such companions thou'ldst unfold, And put in
every honest hand a whip
To lash the rascals naked through the world
Even from the east to the west!

IAGO

Speak within door.

EMILIA

O, fie upon them! Some such squire he was That turn'd your
wit the seamy side without, And made you to suspect me
with the Moor.

IAGO

You are a fool; go to.

DESDEMONA

O good Iago,
What shall I do to win my lord again?
Good friend, go to him; for, by this light of heaven, I know not
how I lost him. Here I kneel:
If e'er my will did trespass 'gainst his love, Either in
discourse of thought or actual deed, Or that mine eyes,
mine ears, or any sense, Delighted them in any other form;
Or that I do not yet, and ever did.
And ever will—though he do shake me off To beggarly
divorcement—love him dearly, Comfort forswear me!
Unkindness may do much; And his unkindness may defeat my
life,
But never taint my love. I cannot say 'whore:'

It does abhor me now I speak the word; To do the act
that might the addition earn

Not the world's mass of vanity could make me.

IAGO

I pray you, be content; 'tis but his humour: The business
of the state does him offence, And he does chide with you.

DESDEMONA

If 'twere no other—

IAGO

'Tis but so, I warrant.

Trumpets within

Hark, how these instruments summon to supper! The
messengers of Venice stay the meat;
Go in, and weep not; all things shall be well. [*Exeunt*

DESDEMONA and EMILIA]

[*Enter RODERIGO*] How now, Roderigo!

RODERIGO

I do not find that thou dealest justly with me.

IAGO

What in the contrary?

RODERIGO

Every day thou daffest me with some device, Iago; and rather, as it seems to
me now, keepest from me all conveniency than suppliest me with the least
advantage of hope. I will indeed no longer endure it, nor am I yet persuaded
to put up in peace what

already I have foolishly suffered.

IAGO

Will you hear me, Roderigo?

RODERIGO

'Faith, I have heard too much, for your words and performances are no kin together.

IAGO

You charge me most unjustly.

RODERIGO

With nought but truth. I have wasted myself out of my means. The jewels you have had from me to deliver to Desdemona would half have corrupted a votarist: you have told me she hath received them and returned me expectations and comforts of sudden respect and acquaintance, but I find none.

IAGO

Well; go to; very well.

RODERIGO

Very well! go to! I cannot go to, man; nor 'tis not very well: nay, I think it is scurvy, and begin to find myself fobbed in it.

IAGO

Very well.

RODERIGO

I tell you 'tis not very well. I will make myself known to Desdemona: if she will return me my jewels, I will give over my suit and repent my unlawful solicitation; if not, assure yourself I will seek satisfaction of you.

IAGO

You have said now.

RODERIGO

Ay, and said nothing but what I protest intendment of doing.

IAGO

Why, now I see there's mettle in thee, and even from this instant to build on thee a better opinion than ever before. Give me thy hand, Roderigo: thou hast taken against me a most just exception; but yet, I protest, I have dealt most directly in thy affair.

RODERIGO

It hath not appeared.

IAGO

I grant indeed it hath not appeared, and your suspicion is not without wit and judgment. But, Roderigo, if thou hast that in thee indeed, which I have greater reason to believe now than ever, I mean purpose, courage and valour, this night show it: if thou the next night following enjoy not Desdemona, take me from this world with treachery and devise engines for my life.

RODERIGO

Well, what is it? is it within reason and compass?

IAGO

Sir, there is especial commission come from Venice to depute Cassio in Othello's place.

RODERIGO

Is that true? why, then Othello and Desdemona return again to
Venice.

IAGO

O, no; he goes into Mauritania and takes away with him the fair
Desdemona, unless his abode be lingered here by some accident: wherein
none can be so determinate as the removing of Cassio.

RODERIGO

How do you mean, removing of him?

IAGO

Why, by making him uncapable of Othello's place; knocking out his
brains.

RODERIGO

And that you would have me to do?

IAGO

Ay, if you dare do yourself a profit and a right. He sups to– night with a
harlotry, and thither will I go to him: he knows not yet of his horrorable
fortune. If you will watch his going thence, which I will fashion to fall out
between twelve and one, you
may take him at your pleasure: I will be near to second your attempt, and he
shall fall between us. Come, stand not amazed at it, but go along with me; I
will show you such a necessity in his death that you shall think yourself
bound to put it on him. It is now high suppertime, and the night grows to
waste: about it.

RODERIGO

I will hear further reason for this.

IAGO

And you shall be satisfied. [*Exeunt*]

Scene III

Another Room in the Castle

[*Enter OTHELLO, LODOVICO, DESDEMONA, EMILIA and Attendants*]

LODOVICO

I do beseech you, sir, trouble yourself no further.

OTHELLO

O, pardon me: 'twill do me good to walk.

LODOVICO

Madam, good night; I humbly thank your ladyship.

DESDEMONA

Your honour is most welcome.

OTHELLO

Will you walk, sir? O,—
Desdemona,—

DESDEMONA

My lord?

OTHELLO

Get you to bed on the instant; I will be returned forthwith:
dismiss your attendant there: look it be done.

DESDEMONA

I will, my lord.

[*Exeunt OTHELLO, LODOVICO, and Attendants*]

EMILIA

How goes it now? he looks gentler than he did.

DESDEMONA

He says he will return incontinent:
He hath commanded me to go to bed, And bade me
to dismiss you.

EMILIA

Dismiss me!

DESDEMONA

It was his bidding: therefore, good Emilia,. Give me my
nightly wearing, and adieu: We must not now displease
him.

EMILIA

I would you had never seen him!

DESDEMONA

So would not I my love doth so approve him,
That even his stubbornness, his cheques, his frowns— Prithee,
unpin me,—have grace and favour in them.

EMILIA

I have laid those sheets you bade me on the bed.

DESDEMONA

All's one. Good faith, how foolish are our minds! If I do die
before thee prithee, shroud me
In one of those same sheets.

EMILIA

Come, come you talk.

DESDEMONA

My mother had a maid call'd Barbara:
She was in love, and he she loved proved mad And did
forsake her: she had a song of 'willow;' An old thing 'twas,
but it express'd her fortune, And she died singing it: that song
to–night
Will not go from my mind; I have much to do, But to go
hang my head all at one side,
And sing it like poor Barbara. Prithee, dispatch.

EMILIA

Shall I go fetch your night–gown?

DESDEMONA

No, unpin me here.
This Lodovico is a proper man.

EMILIA

A very handsome man.

DESDEMONA

He speaks well.

EMILIA

I know a lady in Venice would have walked barefoot to
Palestine for a touch of his nether lip.

DESDEMONA

[Singing] The poor soul sat sighing by a sycamore tree, Sing all a
green willow:
Her hand on her bosom, her head on her knee, Sing willow,
willow, willow:
The fresh streams ran by her, and murmur'd her moans; Sing willow,
willow, willow;
Her salt tears fell from her, and soften'd the stones; Lay by
these:—

Singing

Sing willow, willow, willow; Prithee, hie thee;
he'll come anon:—

Singing

Sing all a green willow must be my garland. Let nobody
blame him; his scorn I approve,–
Nay, that's not next.—Hark! who is't that knocks?

EMILIA

It's the wind.

DESDEMONA

[Singing] I call'd my love false love; but what said he then? Sing willow,
willow, willow: If I court moe women, you'll
couch with moe men! So, get thee gone; good night Ate eyes do itch; Doth
that bode weeping?

EMILIA

'Tis neither here nor there.

DESDEMONA

I have heard it said so. O, these men, these men! Dost thou in
conscience think,—tell me, Emilia,— That there be women do
abuse their husbands
In such gross kind?

EMILIA

There be some such, no question.

DESDEMONA

Wouldst thou do such a deed for all the world?

EMILIA

Why, would not you?

DESDEMONA

No, by this heavenly light!

EMILIA

Nor I neither by this heavenly light; I might do't
as well i' the dark.

DESDEMONA

Wouldst thou do such a deed for all the world?

EMILIA

The world's a huge thing: it is a great price. For a small
vice.

DESDEMONA

In troth, I think thou wouldst not.

EMILIA

In troth, I think I should; and undo't when I had done. Marry, I would not do such a thing for a joint–ring, nor for measures of lawn, nor for gowns, petticoats, nor caps, nor any petty exhibition; but for the whole world,— why, who would not make her husband a cuckold to make him a monarch? I should venture purgatory for't.

DESDEMONA

Beshrew me, if I would do such a wrong
For the whole world.

EMILIA

Why the wrong is but a wrong i' the world: and having the world for your labour, tis a wrong in your own world, and you might quickly make it right.

DESDEMONA

I do not think there is any such woman.

EMILIA

Yes, a dozen; and as many to the vantage as would store the world they played for. But I do think it is their husbands' faults If wives do fall: say that they slack their duties, And pour our treasures into foreign laps, Or else break out in peevish jealousies, Throwing restraint upon us; or say they strike us, Or scant our former having in despite; Why, we have galls, and though we have some grace, Yet have we some revenge. Let husbands know Their wives have sense like them: they see and smell And have their palates both for sweet and sour, As husbands have. What is it that they do When they change us for others? Is it sport? I think it is: and doth affection breed it? I think it doth: is't frailty that thus errs? It is so too: and have not we affections, Desires for sport, and frailty, as men have? Then let them use us well: else let them know, The ills we do, their ills instruct us so.

DESDEMONA

Good night, good night: heaven me such uses send, Not to pick bad from bad, but by bad mend!

[*Exeunt*]

ACT V

Scene I

Cyprus. a Street

[Enter IAGO and RODERIGO]

IAGO

> Here, stand behind this bulk; straight will he come: Wear thy
> good rapier bare, and put it home:
> Quick, quick; fear nothing; I'll be at thy elbow: It makes us,
> or it mars us; think on that,
> And fix most firm thy resolution.

RODERIGO

> Be near at hand; I may miscarry in't.

IAGO

> Here, at thy hand: be bold, and take thy stand.

Retires

RODERIGO

> I have no great devotion to the deed;
> And yet he hath given me satisfying reasons:
> 'Tis but a man gone. Forth, my sword: he dies.

IAGO

> I have rubb'd this young quat almost to the sense, And he grows
> angry. Now, whether he kill Cassio, Or Cassio him, or each do
> kill the other,

Every way makes my gain: live Roderigo, He calls me
to a restitution large
Of gold and jewels that I bobb'd from him, As gifts to
Desdemona;
It must not be: if Cassio do remain, He hath a
daily beauty in his life
That makes me ugly; and, besides, the Moor
May unfold me to him; there stand I in much peril: No, he must
die. But so: I hear him coming.

[Enter CASSIO]

RODERIGO

I know his gait, 'tis he.—Villain, thou diest!

Makes a pass at CASSIO

CASSIO

That thrust had been mine enemy indeed, But that my
coat is better than thou know'st I will make proof of
thine.

Draws, and wounds RODERIGO

RODERIGO

O, I am slain!

IAGO from behind wounds CASSIO in the leg, and exit

CASSIO

I am maim'd for ever. Help, ho! murder! murder!

Falls

[Enter OTHELLO]

OTHELLO

The voice of Cassio: Iago keeps his word.

RODERIGO

O, villain that I am!

OTHELLO

It is even so.

CASSIO

O, help, ho! light! a surgeon!

OTHELLO

'Tis he:—O brave Iago, honest and just,
That hast such noble sense of thy friend's wrong! Thou
teachest me. Minion, your dear lies dead, And your unblest
fate hies: strumpet, I come.
Forth of my heart those charms, thine eyes, are blotted; Thy bed,
lust–stain'd, shall with lust's blood be spotted.

[*Exit*]

[*Enter LODOVICO and GRATIANO*]

CASSIO

What, ho! no watch? no passage? murder! murder!

GRATIANO

'Tis some mischance; the cry is very direful.

CASSIO

O, help!

LODOVICO

Hark!

RODERIGO

O wretched villain!

LODOVICO

Two or three groan: it is a heavy night:
These may be counterfeits: let's think't unsafe
To come in to the cry without more help.

RODERIGO

Nobody come? then shall I bleed to death.

LODOVICO

Hark!

Re–enter IAGO, with a light

GRATIANO

Here's one comes in his shirt, with light and weapons.

IAGO

Who's there? whose noise is this that ones on murder?

LODOVICO

We do not know.

IAGO

Did not you hear a cry?

CASSIO

Here, here! for heaven's sake, help me!

IAGO

What's the matter?

GRATIANO

This is Othello's ancient, as I take it.

LODOVICO

The same indeed; a very valiant fellow.

IAGO

What are you here that cry so grievously?

CASSIO

Iago? O, I am spoil'd, undone by villains! Give me some help.

IAGO

O me, lieutenant! what villains have done this?

CASSIO

I think that one of them is hereabout, And cannot make away.

IAGO

O treacherous villains!
What are you there? come in, and give some help.

To LODOVICO and GRATIANO

RODERIGO

O, help me here!

CASSIO

That's one of them.

IAGO

O murderous slave! O villain!

Stabs RODERIGO

RODERIGO

O damn'd Iago! O inhuman dog!

IAGO

Kill men i' the dark!—Where be these bloody thieves?— How silent is
this town!—Ho! murder! murder!—
What may you be? are you of good or evil?

LODOVICO

As you shall prove us, praise us.

IAGO

Signior Lodovico?

LODOVICO

He, sir.

IAGO

I cry you mercy. Here's Cassio hurt by villains.

GRATIANO

Cassio!

IAGO

How is't, brother!

CASSIO

My leg is cut in two.

IAGO

Marry, heaven forbid!
Light, gentlemen; I'll bind it with my shirt. [*Enter*

BIANCA]

BIANCA

What is the matter, ho? who is't that cried?

IAGO

Who is't that cried!

BIANCA

O my dear Cassio! my sweet Cassio! O Cassio, Cassio,
Cassio!

IAGO

O notable strumpet! Cassio, may you suspect
Who they should be that have thus many led you?

CASSIO

No.

GRATIANO

I am to find you thus: I have been to seek you.

IAGO

Lend me a garter. So. O, for a chair, To bear him
easily hence!

BIANCA

Alas, he faints! O Cassio, Cassio, Cassio!

IAGO

Gentlemen all, I do suspect this trash
To be a party in this injury.
Patience awhile, good Cassio. Come, come; Lend me a
light. Know we this face or no? Alas my friend and my
dear countryman
Roderigo! no:—yes, sure: O heaven! Roderigo.

GRATIANO

What, of Venice?

IAGO

Even he, sir; did you know him?

GRATIANO

Know him! ay.

IAGO

Signior Gratiano? I cry you gentle pardon;
These bloody accidents must excuse my manners, That so
neglected you.

GRATIANO

I am glad to see you.

IAGO

How do you, Cassio? O, a chair, a chair!

GRATIANO

Roderigo!

IAGO

He, he 'tis he.

A chair brought in

O, that's well said; the chair!

GRATIANO

Some good man bear him carefully from hence; I'll fetch the
general's surgeon.

To BIANCA

For you, mistress, Save you your labour. He that lies slain here, Cassio, Was
my dear friend: what malice was between you?

CASSIO

None in the world; nor do I know the man.

IAGO

[To BIANCA] What, look you pale? O, bear him out o' the air.

CASSIO and RODERIGO are borne off

Stay you, good gentlemen. Look you pale, mistress? Do you
perceive the gastness of her eye?
Nay, if you stare, we shall hear more anon. Behold her
well; I pray you, look upon her:

Do you see, gentlemen? nay, guiltiness will speak, Though tongues were out of use.

[*Enter EMILIA*]

EMILIA

'Las, what's the matter? what's the matter, husband?

IAGO

Cassio hath here been set on in the dark By Roderigo and fellows that are scaped: He's almost slain, and Roderigo dead.

EMILIA

Alas, good gentleman! alas, good Cassio!

IAGO

This is the fruit of whoring. Prithee, Emilia, Go know of Cassio where he supp'd to–night.

To BIANCA

What, do you shake at that?

BIANCA

He supp'd at my house; but I therefore shake not.

IAGO

O, did he so? I charge you, go with me.

EMILIA

Fie, fie upon thee, strumpet!

BIANCA

> I am no strumpet; but of life as honest
> As you that thus abuse me.

EMILIA

> As I! foh! fie upon thee!

IAGO

> Kind gentlemen, let's go see poor Cassio dress'd. Come,
> mistress, you must tell's another tale. Emilia run you to the
> citadel,
> And tell my lord and lady what hath happ'd. Will you go
> on? I pray.

Aside

> This is the night
> That either makes me or fordoes me quite. [*Exeunt*]

Scene II

A Bedchamber in the Castle: Desdemona in Bed Asleep;

a light burning. [*Enter*

OTHELLO] **OTHELLO**

It is the cause, it is the cause, my soul,——
Let me not name it to you, you chaste stars!— It is the
cause. Yet I'll not shed her blood;
Nor scar that whiter skin of hers than snow, And smooth
as monumental alabaster.
Yet she must die, else she'll betray more men. Put out the
light, and then put out the light:
If I quench thee, thou flaming minister, I can again
thy former light restore,
Should I repent me: but once put out thy light, Thou
cunning'st pattern of excelling nature,
I know not where is that Promethean heat
That can thy light relume. When I have pluck'd the rose, I cannot give
it vital growth again.
It must needs wither: I'll smell it on the tree.

Kissing her

Ah balmy breath, that dost almost persuade Justice to break
her sword! One more, one more. Be thus when thou art dead,
and I will kill thee, And love thee after. One more, and this the
last: So sweet was ne'er so fatal. I must weep,
But they are cruel tears: this sorrow's heavenly;

It strikes where it doth love. She wakes.

DESDEMONA

Who's there? Othello?

OTHELLO

Ay. Desdemona.

DESDEMONA

Will you come to bed, my lord?

OTHELLO

Have you pray'd to–night, Desdemona?

DESDEMONA

Ay, my lord.

OTHELLO

If you bethink yourself of any crime Unreconciled as
yet to heaven and grace, Solicit for it straight.

DESDEMONA

Alas, my lord, what do you mean by that?

OTHELLO

Well, do it, and be brief; I will walk by: I would not
kill thy unprepared spirit;
No; heaven forfend! I would not kill thy soul.

DESDEMONA

Talk you of killing?

OTHELLO

Ay, I do.

DESDEMONA

Then heaven
Have mercy on me!

OTHELLO

Amen, with all my heart!

DESDEMONA

If you say so, I hope you will not kill me.

OTHELLO

Hum!

DESDEMONA

And yet I fear you; for you are fatal then
When your eyes roll so: why I should fear I know not, Since
guiltiness I know not; but yet I feel I fear.

OTHELLO

Think on thy sins.

DESDEMONA

They are loves I bear to you.

OTHELLO

Ay, and for that thou diest.

DESDEMONA

That death's unnatural that kills for loving. Alas, why
gnaw you so your nether lip?
Some bloody passion shakes your very frame: These are
portents; but yet I hope, I hope, They do not point on me.

OTHELLO

Peace, and be still!

DESDEMONA

I will so. What's the matter?

OTHELLO

That handkerchief which I so loved and gave thee
Thou gavest to Cassio.

DESDEMONA

No, by my life and soul!
Send for the man, and ask him.

OTHELLO

Sweet soul, take heed,
Take heed of perjury; thou art on thy deathbed.

DESDEMONA

Ay, but not yet to die.

OTHELLO

Yes, presently:
Therefore confess thee freely of thy sin;

For to deny each article with oath
Cannot remove nor choke the strong conception
That I do groan withal. Thou art to die.

DESDEMONA

Then Lord have mercy on me!

OTHELLO

I say, amen.

DESDEMONA

And have you mercy too! I never did Offend you in my
life; never loved Cassio But with such general warranty
of heaven As I might love: I never gave him token.

OTHELLO

By heaven, I saw my handkerchief in's hand. O perjured
woman! thou dost stone my heart, And makest me call what
I intend to do
A murder, which I thought a sacrifice: I saw the
handkerchief.

DESDEMONA

He found it then;
I never gave it him: send for him hither; Let him
confess a truth.

OTHELLO

He hath confess'd.

DESDEMONA

What, my lord?

OTHELLO

That he hath used thee.

DESDEMONA

How? unlawfully?

OTHELLO

Ay.

DESDEMONA

He will not say so.

OTHELLO

No, his mouth is stopp'd;
Honest Iago hath ta'en order for't.

DESDEMONA

O! my fear interprets: what, is he dead?

OTHELLO

Had all his hairs been lives, my great revenge
Had stomach for them all.

DESDEMONA

Alas! he is betray'd and I undone.

OTHELLO

Out, strumpet! weep'st thou for him to my face?

DESDEMONA

O, banish me, my lord, but kill me not!

OTHELLO

Down, strumpet!

DESDEMONA

Kill me to–morrow: let me live to–night!

OTHELLO

Nay, if you strive—

DESDEMONA

But half an hour!

OTHELLO

Being done, there is no pause.

DESDEMONA

But while I say one prayer!

OTHELLO

It is too late. *He stifles her*

EMILIA

[Within] My lord , my lord! what, ho! my lord, my lord!

OTHELLO

What noise is this? Not dead? not yet quite dead? I that am
cruel am yet merciful;
I would not have thee linger in thy pain: So, so.

EMILIA

[Within] What, ho! my lord, my lord!

OTHELLO

Who's there?

EMILIA

[Within] O, good my lord, I would speak a word with you!

OTHELLO

Yes: 'tis Emilia. By and by. She's dead.
'Tis like she comes to speak of Cassio's death.— The noise
was here. Ha! no more moving?
Still as the grave. Shall she come in? were't good?— I think she
stirs again:—no. What's best to do?
If she come in, she'll sure speak to my wife: My wife! my
wife! what wife? I have no wife. O insupportable! O heavy
hour!
Methinks it should be now a huge eclipse
Of sun and moon, and that the affrighted globe
Should yawn at alteration.

EMILIA

[Within] I do beseech you
That I may speak with you, O, good my lord!

OTHELLO

I had forgot thee: O, come in, Emilia;
Soft; by and by. Let me the curtains draw. Where art
thou?

Unlocks the door

[*Enter EMILIA*] What's the matter with thee now?

EMILIA

O, my good lord, yonder's foul murders done!

OTHELLO

What, now?

EMILIA

But now, my lord.

OTHELLO

It is the very error of the moon;
She comes more nearer earth than she was wont, And makes
men mad.

EMILIA

Cassio, my lord, hath kill'd a young Venetian
Call'd Roderigo.

OTHELLO

Roderigo kill'd! And Cassio
kill'd!

EMILIA

No, Cassio is not kill'd.

OTHELLO

Not Cassio kill'd! then murder's out of tune, And sweet
revenge grows harsh.

DESDEMONA

O, falsely, falsely murder'd!

EMILIA

Alas, what cry is that?

OTHELLO

That! what?

EMILIA

Out, and alas! that was my lady's voice. Help! help, ho!
help! O lady, speak again! Sweet Desdemona! O sweet
mistress, speak!

DESDEMONA

A guiltless death I die.

EMILIA

O, who hath done this deed?

DESDEMONA

Nobody; I myself. Farewell
Commend me to my kind lord: O, farewell!

Dies

OTHELLO

Why, how should she be murder'd?

EMILIA

Alas, who knows?

OTHELLO

You heard her say herself, it was not I.

EMILIA

She said so: I must needs report the truth.

OTHELLO

She's, like a liar, gone to burning hell:
'Twas I that kill'd her.

EMILIA

O, the more angel she,
And you the blacker devil!

OTHELLO

She turn'd to folly, and she was a whore.

EMILIA

Thou dost belie her, and thou art a devil.

OTHELLO

She was false as water.

EMILIA

Thou art rash as fire, to say
That she was false: O, she was heavenly true!

OTHELLO

Cassio did top her; ask thy husband else. O, I were
damn'd beneath all depth in hell, But that I did proceed
upon just grounds
To this extremity. Thy husband knew it all.

EMILIA

My husband!

OTHELLO

Thy husband.

EMILIA

That she was false to wedlock?

OTHELLO

Ay, with Cassio. Nay, had she been true,
If heaven would make me such another world
Of one entire and Perfect chrysolite, I'ld not have
sold her for it.

EMILIA

My husband!

OTHELLO

Ay, 'twas he that told me first:
An honest man he is, and hates the slime
That sticks on filthy deeds.

EMILIA

My husband!

OTHELLO

What needs this iteration, woman? I say thy husband.

EMILIA

O mistress, villany hath made mocks with love,

My husband say that she was false!

OTHELLO

He, woman;
I say thy husband: dost understand the word? My friend,
thy husband, honest, honest Iago.

EMILIA

If he say so, may his pernicious soul
Rot half a grain a day! he lies to the heart: She was too
fond of her most filthy bargain.

OTHELLO

Ha!

EMILIA

Do thy worst:
This deed of thine is no more worthy heaven
Than thou wast worthy her.

OTHELLO

Peace, you were best.

EMILIA

Thou hast not half that power to do me harm
As I have to be hurt. O gull! O dolt!
As ignorant as dirt! thou hast done a deed—
I care not for thy sword; I'll make thee known, Though I lost
twenty lives.—Help! help, ho! help! The Moor hath kill'd my
mistress! Murder! murder!

[*Enter MONTANO, GRATIANO, IAGO, and others*]

MONTANO

What is the matter? How now, general!

EMILIA

O, are you come, Iago? you have done well, That men must lay their murders on your neck.

GRATIANO

What is the matter?

EMILIA

Disprove this villain, if thou be'st a man:
He says thou told'st him that his wife was false: I know thou didst not, thou'rt not such a villain: Speak, for my heart is full.

IAGO

I told him what I thought, and told no more
Than what he found himself was apt and true.

EMILIA

But did you ever tell him she was false?

IAGO

I did.

EMILIA

You told a lie, an odious, damned lie; Upon my soul, a lie, a wicked lie.
She false with Cassio!—did you say with Cassio?

IAGO

With Cassio, mistress. Go to, charm your tongue.

EMILIA

I will not charm my tongue; I am bound to speak: My mistress
here lies murder'd in her bed,—

All

O heavens forfend!

EMILIA

And your reports have set the murder on.

OTHELLO

Nay, stare not, masters: it is true, indeed.

GRATIANO

'Tis a strange truth.

MONTANO

O monstrous act!

EMILIA

Villany, villany, villany!
I think upon't, I think: I smell't: O villany!—
I thought so then:—I'll kill myself for grief:— O villany,
villany!

IAGO

What, are you mad? I charge you, get you home.

EMILIA

Good gentlemen, let me have leave to speak:
'Tis proper I obey him, but not now. Perchance,
Iago, I will ne'er go home.

OTHELLO

O! O! O!

He falls on the bed

EMILIA

Nay, lay thee down and roar;
For thou hast kill'd the sweetest innocent
That e'er did lift up eye.

OTHELLO

[Rising] O, she was foul!
I scarce did know you, uncle: there lies your niece, Whose breath,
indeed, these hands have newly stopp'd: I know this act shows
horrible and grim.

GRATIANO

Poor Desdemona! I am glad thy father's dead: Thy match was
mortal to him, and pure grief Shore his old thread in twain:
did he live now, This sight would make him do a desperate
turn, Yea, curse his better angel from his side,
And fall to reprobation.

OTHELLO

'Tis pitiful; but yet Iago knows
That she with Cassio hath the act of shame
A thousand times committed; Cassio confess'd it: And she did
gratify his amorous works

With that recognizance and pledge of love Which I first
gave her; I saw it in his hand: It was a handkerchief, an
antique token
My father gave my mother.

EMILIA

O heaven! O heavenly powers!

IAGO

Come, hold your peace.

EMILIA

'Twill out, 'twill out: I peace!
No, I will speak as liberal as the north:
Let heaven and men and devils, let them all, All, all, cry
shame against me, yet I'll speak.

IAGO

Be wise, and get you home.

EMILIA

I will not.

IAGO offers to stab EMILIA

GRATIANO

Fie!
Your sword upon a woman?

EMILIA

O thou dull Moor! that handkerchief thou speak'st of
I found by fortune and did give my husband;

For often, with a solemn earnestness,
More than indeed belong'd to such a trifle, He begg'd of
me to steal it.

IAGO

Villanous whore!

EMILIA

She give it Cassio! no, alas! I found it, And I did
give't my husband.

IAGO

Filth, thou liest!

EMILIA

By heaven, I do not, I do not, gentlemen.
O murderous coxcomb! what should such a fool
Do with so good a woman?

OTHELLO

Are there no stones in heaven
But what serve for the thunder?—Precious villain!

He runs at IAGO IAGO, from behind, stabs EMILIA, and exit

GRATIANO

The woman falls; sure, he hath kill'd his wife.

EMILIA

Ay, ay: O, lay me by my mistress' side.

GRATIANO

He's gone, but his wife's kill'd.

MONTANO

'Tis a notorious villain. Take you this weapon, Which I have
here recover'd from the Moor: Come, guard the door without;
let him not pass, But kill him rather. I'll after that same
villain, For 'tis a damned slave.

[*Exeunt MONTANO and GRATIANO*]

OTHELLO

I am not valiant neither,
But ever puny whipster gets my sword: But why
should honour outlive honesty? Let it go all.

EMILIA

What did thy song bode, lady?
Hark, canst thou hear me? I will play the swan. And die in
music.

Singing

Willow, willow, willow,—
Moor, she was chaste; she loved thee, cruel Moor; So come my
soul to bliss, as I speak true;
So speaking as I think, I die, I die.

Dies

OTHELLO

I have another weapon in this chamber;
It is a sword of Spain, the ice–brook's temper:—

O, here it is. Uncle, I must come forth.

GRATIANO

[Within] If thou attempt it, it will cost thee dear: Thou hast no
weapon, and perforce must suffer.

OTHELLO

Look in upon me then and speak with me, Or, naked as
I am, I will assault thee.

Re–enter GRATIANO

GRATIANO

What is the matter?

OTHELLO

Behold, I have a weapon;
A better never did itself sustain
Upon a soldier's thigh: I have seen the day, That, with this
little arm and this good sword,
I have made my way through more impediments Than twenty
times your stop: but, O vain boast! Who can control his fate?
'tis not so now.
Be not afraid, though you do see me weapon'd; Here is my
journey's end, here is my butt,
And very sea–mark of my utmost sail.
Do you go back dismay'd? 'tis a lost fear; Man but a
rush against Othello's breast, And he retires. Where
should Othello go?
Now, how dost thou look now? O ill–starr'd wench! Pale as thy
smock! when we shall meet at compt, This look of thine will hurl
my soul from heaven, And fiends will snatch at it. Cold, cold, my
girl! Even like thy chastity. O cursed slave!

Whip me, ye devils,
From the possession of this heavenly sight! Blow me about
in winds! roast me in sulphur! Wash me in steep–down
gulfs of liquid fire!
O Desdemona! Desdemona! dead! Oh! Oh! Oh!

[*Enter LODOVICO. MONTANO, CASSIO carried in a chair, and
Officers with IAGO, prisoner*]

LODOVICO

Where is this rash and most unfortunate man?

OTHELLO

That's he that was Othello: here I am.

LODOVICO

Where is that viper? bring the villain forth.

OTHELLO

I look down towards his feet; but that's a fable. If that thou
best a devil, I cannot kill thee.

Wounds IAGO

LODOVICO

Wrench his sword from him.

IAGO

I bleed, sir; but not kill'd.

OTHELLO

I am not sorry neither: I'ld have thee live;

For, in my sense, 'tis happiness to die.

LODOVICO

O thou Othello, thou wert once so good, Fall'n in the
practise of a damned slave, What shall be said to thee?

OTHELLO

Why, any thing:
An honourable murderer, if you will;
For nought I did in hate, but all in honour.

LODOVICO

This wretch hath part confess'd his villany: Did you and
he consent in Cassio's death?

OTHELLO

Ay.

CASSIO

Dear general, I never gave you cause.

OTHELLO

I do believe it, and I ask your pardon. Will you, I pray,
demand that demi–devil
Why he hath thus ensnared my soul and body?

IAGO

Demand me nothing: what you know, you know: From this
time forth I never will speak word.

LODOVICO

What, not to pray?

GRATIANO

Torments will ope your lips.

OTHELLO

Well, thou dost best.

LODOVICO

Sir, you shall understand what hath befall'n, Which, as I
think, you know not. Here is a letter Found in the pocket of
the slain Roderigo;
And here another: the one of them imports
The death of Cassio to be undertook
By Roderigo.

OTHELLO

O villain!

CASSIO

Most heathenish and most gross!

LODOVICO

Now here's another discontented paper, Found in his pocket
too; and this, it seems, Roderigo meant to have sent this
damned villain; But that belike Iago in the interim
Came in and satisfied him.

OTHELLO

O the pernicious caitiff!
How came you, Cassio, by that handkerchief

That was my wife's?

CASSIO

I found it in my chamber:
And he himself confess'd but even now
That there he dropp'd it for a special purpose
Which wrought to his desire.

OTHELLO

O fool! fool! fool!

CASSIO

There is besides in Roderigo's letter, How he upbraids
Iago, that he made him Brave me upon the watch;
whereon it came That I was cast: and even but now he
spake, After long seeming dead, Iago hurt him, Iago set
him on.

LODOVICO

You must forsake this room, and go with us: Your power
and your command is taken off, And Cassio rules in
Cyprus. For this slave,
If there be any cunning cruelty
That can torment him much and hold him long, It shall be
his. You shall close prisoner rest,
Till that the nature of your fault be known
To the Venetian state. Come, bring him away.

OTHELLO

Soft you; a word or two before you go.
I have done the state some service, and they know't. No more of
that. I pray you, in your letters,

When you shall these unlucky deeds relate, Speak of me
as I am; nothing extenuate,
Nor set down aught in malice: then must you speak
Of one that loved not wisely but too well;
Of one not easily jealous, but being wrought Perplex'd in
the extreme; of one whose hand, Like the base Indian, threw
a pearl away
Richer than all his tribe; of one whose subdued eyes, Albeit
unused to the melting mood,
Drop tears as fast as the Arabian trees Their medicinal
gum. Set you down this; And say besides, that in
Aleppo once, Where a malignant and a turban'd Turk
Beat a Venetian and traduced the state,
I took by the throat the circumcised dog, And smote
him, thus.

Stabs himself

LODOVICO

O bloody period!

GRATIANO

All that's spoke is marr'd.

OTHELLO

I kiss'd thee ere I kill'd thee: no way but this; Killing
myself, to die upon a kiss.

Falls on the bed, and dies

CASSIO

This did I fear, but thought he had no weapon; For he was
great of heart.

LODOVICO

[To IAGO] O Spartan dog,
More fell than anguish, hunger, or the sea! Look on the
tragic loading of this bed;
This is thy work: the object poisons sight; Let it be hid.
Gratiano, keep the house, And seize upon the fortunes
of the Moor,
For they succeed on you. To you, lord governor, Remains the
censure of this hellish villain;
The time, the place, the torture: O, enforce it! Myself will
straight aboard: and to the state This heavy act with heavy
heart relate.

Printed in Great Britain
by Amazon

26757767R00118